Duck Island

Also by Steve Weiner

The Museum of Love
The Yellow Sailor
Sweet England

Duck Island

Steve Weiner

VANCOUVER
NEW STAR BOOKS
2023

NEW STAR BOOKS LTD
No. 107–3477 Commercial St
Vancouver, BC V5N 4E8 CANADA
1574 Gulf Road, No. 1517
Point Roberts, WA 98281 USA
newstarbooks.com . info@newstarbooks.com

The publisher acknowledges the financial support of the Canada Council for the Arts, the British Columbia Arts Council, and the Government of Canada.
Nous reconnaissons l'appui financier du gouvernement du Canada.

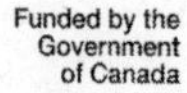

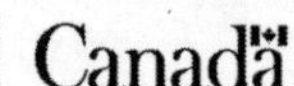

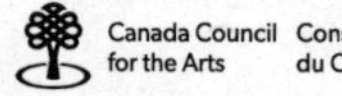

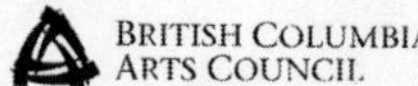

Supported by the Province of British Columbia

Cataloguing information for this book is available from Library and Archives Canada, www.collectionscanada.gc.ca.
ISBN: 978-1-55420-203-4

Cover design by Oliver McPartlin
Typeset by New Star Books in Utopia Std and Helvetica Neue
Printed and bound in Canada by Imprimerie Gauvin, Gatineau, QC
First printing November 2023

Acknowledgements

John Lang
Debbi Weiner
Elton Stone
Jim Smit
Mark Weiner

Duck Island

It's real to them that believe.

— Doc Watson

Chapter 1

It was the house of Chris Carsten alright, but something was wrong. Cal Bedrick pressed the white doorbell anyway. Mrs. Carsten, a slightly plump middle-aged lady with brown hair and freckles, opened the door. She stared at him for a while.

"Oh my, Cal Bedrick! I barely recognized you. Chris isn't here, she's in Stevens Point, but please do come in. We can have a chat."

Cal went inside.

On the left was the bedroom which Chris had once shared with her older sister Cathy. There was a redwood bunk bed, a small desk, and a deep but empty closet. Winter coats hung from pegs beside the door. The floor was wood, and the window looked out onto the neighbor's garden. Further on the left was Randy's bedroom. The door was closed.

Cal walked ahead. There was a long aquarium in the corridor with a very long crack running through the glass. It still held water, and there were still fish in it. Straight ahead was the parents' bedroom with a tufted appliqué quilt. Just to the right before the parents' bedroom was a black-and-white photograph of Chris. She must have been about eight years old at the time and very cute. Her hair was brilliant white and straight with bangs. She had been a safety guard and had won a trip to Washington, D.C. There were no photographs of the other three children.

They went into the living room and sat on opposing green vinyl easy chairs. Behind Mrs. Carsten was a large plate glass window overlooking a well-trimmed green lawn and a pink gravel alley.

"Looking at your trousers, Cal, and your shoes, I can tell you've been doing some hard traveling."

Cal grinned. “Yes, Mrs. Carsten.”

“Please, call me Margaret. Where have you been?”

“The West Coast.”

“Have you committed any crimes? Is anybody chasing you?”

“Do I really look that bad?”

Margaret laughed. “Yes, you do.”

“Well, it’s been four years since I left home.”

There was a moment of silence.

“Margaret, why is Chris in Stevens Point? She went to Macalester College in Minnesota.”

“She got a job with the Stevens Point Park Service making art for the park system. She lives with a housemate named Eva.”

“Is she married?”

“No. She almost married a Jewish fellow, but it broke apart the day before the wedding.”

“What happened?”

“We never knew.”

There was a pause.

“Where are you staying, Cal?” Margaret asked.

“Duck Island.”

Margaret made a face of sympathy. “There is no place to stay there.”

“I know, but that’s where I’m staying.”

“Please, Cal, stay here. You can sleep in Chris’s bed.”

“Oh no, I could never do that.”

The door to Randy’s room opened. Randy came out. He was around fourteen years old. His knuckles were heavily bandaged. He came into the living room and leaned against his mother.

“Mommy, I’m hungry,” he whined.

“Have you had anything to eat, Cal?” Margaret asked

“No, not really.”

“Please, stay for lunch. I’ll call Phil, and he’ll join us.”

She went to the telephone and called her husband.

“Phil, you remember Cal Bedrick, don’t you? The boy who followed Chris home everyday and drove her nuts? He’s here, and I’ve invited him for lunch. Would you come home? I’ll heat up the meatloaf.”

They hung up. Margaret spread a white tablecloth on the dining room table, which was in front of a dark mahogany hutch. She spread four plates and four sets of cutlery on cloth napkins, laid out four glasses, and put a basket of bread rolls in the middle of the table.

"Please Cal, sit."

Margaret went to the refrigerator and pulled out the meatloaf. She took off the aluminum foil, put the meatloaf in the oven, and set the dial. Then she went to the refrigerator, took out a glass pitcher of orange juice, and brought it to the table. She filled all four glasses.

Randy reached for the bread rolls.

"Mommy, I need butter."

Margaret went to the fridge, brought out the cut glass butter holder, and placed it on the table.

"There's no butter knife," Randy said.

She opened a hutch door, took out a butter knife, and gently buttered a roll for Randy.

"What happened to your knuckles, Randy?" Cal asked.

"I took LSD and chewed them off."

"Why did you do that?"

Randy laughed. "Why do people do anything?"

"It's dangerous, Randy. I happen to know," Cal said.

"Every kid in my class takes this stuff."

A beige Volvo pulled into the driveway. The door opened, and Mr. Phil Carsten came in. He was tall, slender, black-haired, about fifty. He wore a white shirt with a speckled maroon tie and dark, neatly pressed trousers. He moved very neatly. He held out his hand to Cal, who stood to shake it.

"Cal Bedrick, I haven't seen you in donkey's years."

"How nice to see you, Mr. Carsten," Cal said.

Phil gestured to Cal's chair. The stove timer went off.

"Oh, that must be the meatloaf. I'll get it. Margaret, you stay where you are," Phil said.

Phil put a round wicker placemat on the table. He opened the oven door and with oven gloves pulled out the meatloaf. He placed the meatloaf in the glass oven dish onto the placemat.

Margaret handed him a slicing knife.

"Me first," Randy said.

"We have a guest Randy," Phil said.

"It's just Cal."

Phil cut the meatloaf into smaller pieces. He put a slice on Cal's plate then one on Randy's. Phil served Margaret and then himself. Margaret forked a slice and gave it to Randy.

Phil lifted his orange juice. Everybody did the same. They all faced Cal.

"To you, Cal, may your future be good," Phil said.

They all drank.

"They moved the Employers Mutual to the beltline, so I haven't much time."

"Sir, what do you actually do?" Cal asked politely.

"I am the writer-editor of accident prevention media."

"Where's Cathy?" Cal asked.

"She's on a commune in Nebraska," Margaret said.

"Kansas," Randy said.

"She doesn't take drugs though," Phil said.

"Does Chris?" Cal asked.

"God no," Margaret, Phil, and Randy all said together.

"Where's Phil Junior?" Cal asked.

"Margaret, would you get that newspaper article and show it to Cal?" Phil said.

Margaret got a newspaper clipping from a hutch drawer and handed it to Cal.

"That's a photograph of Phil Junior. I would recognize a Carsten anywhere," Cal said.

Phil explained. "There had been a terrible riot in the Toxteth part of Liverpool. Prince Charles came to visit, and Phil Junior carried a sign that read 'Toxteth needs reality, not royalty'."

The odd thing about the article was that the writer went on and on about the cult into which Phil Junior had married. There were alleged sexual improprieties.

"This is a hatchet job to protect the prince from well-deserved criticism," Phil said.

There was a pause.

“Randy, once I get to Stevens Point, where can I find Chris?”

“You cross the river past a brick bakery. Turn left on Second Street. She lives with Eva at number 32. A very pretty yellow and brown bungalow.”

Margaret said, “If you follow an asphalt path to the right of the bungalow, you’ll come to a green wooden clubhouse. That’s where Chris and Eva do their artwork.”

They finished eating.

“I want some Jell-O for dessert,” Randy said.

“Not now, Randy.”

Phil looked at his watch. “I’m sorry, but I have to go already.”

They all walked to the front door. Phil opened it.

There was no green grass. It was all yellow or white. There was one tree, a sapling with three red leaves protected by chicken wire. The garage door was open. Chris’s silver canoe was fixed to the rafters.

“I should really do something about this lawn. It’s a shame of the neighborhood,” Phil said.

Phil offered Cal a twenty-dollar bill.

“Oh no, please, sir, don’t do that,” Cal said.

“Go on, take it. I can tell you’re not wealthy.”

“I don’t accept money from people I visit. Thank you both for a lovely lunch,” Cal said.

“Well, nice to see you, Cal. I hope you get to see Chris. Don’t tell Chris where you got her address,” Phil said as he got into his Volvo. He turned on the ignition, backed up, and with a wave, he drove off.

“Please, please, take Chris and Cathy’s room. It’s clean. It’s warm, and it’s safe,” Margaret said, “and we would like your company. There’s nothing at Duck Island for you.”

Cal shook his head. “Thank you, but I can’t.”

“Chris will never have sex with you,” Randy said.

Margaret clopped Randy on the back of his head.

“Ow!” Randy’s head went down, and his shoulders went up. They went in. The door closed.

Chapter 2

Cal walked to the Stone Street Bridge, crossed the bright silver Wisconsin River, and walked up Stuart Avenue, pausing at the new University of Wisconsin Extension Center. It was much larger than he remembered. He walked until he was on Route 51, the north-south highway, and hitched a ride from a farmer who spoke only with a battery-driven device held firmly against his throat.

His words came out buzzy and hard to decipher. A miniature Wausau Lumberjack dangled from the rear-view mirror. They drove south, parallel to the river.

"*Where are you going, son?*" the farmer buzzed.

"Stevens Point."

"*On business?*"

"Unfinished business."

There was a long, low, greenish-brown hill with clusters of autumn leaves among the pine trees. On the top was a red and white blinking radio transmission tower with a shorter wooden viewing platform. That was Rib Hill, deemed to be the highest point in Wisconsin. The Wausau Chamber of Commerce voted to change the name of Rib Hill to Rib Mountain. To the north, closer to Rhinelander, Timms Hill was found to be a few feet higher than Rib Mountain and thus deemed to be Wisconsin's highest point.

Cal leaned against the front seat upholstery and closed his eyes. He had dreamed about Chris every morning for at least a hundred days in these last four years. He looked out the window as trees half denuded of their leaves passed by and the sun flickered through half bare branches. He prayed for the energy and moral strength to win her. He opened his eyes. On the left was a field already harvested, and below that, a slight slope. The Wisconsin River was dark purple in the sun with silvery currents and dark eddies racing forward to a bridge before downtown Stevens Point.

The highway was black with a white dashed line in the center. As it curved, there was the illusion of it going left, going right, going left, going right, but when the farmer got to those points, the road was straight. There were optical illusions, mirages of large silvery puddles on the road ahead, but when the farmer got there they disappeared. There was only the deep black highway with a white line dashed down the center.

On the right was the farm, so the sign said, of Gustav Bardy, who collected blue things. Two broken blue cars were in his driveway. He grew blueberries, painted his front door blue, and had a blue Virgin Mary on the porch. The fence to the pig pen was also painted blue.

They passed two silver silos. A group of wide-eyed cows watched the farmer drive by. On the right behind Gustav Bardy's blue farm was a small airport with one single-wing propeller aircraft revving up. On a ridge was a line of green-black pine trees that made a small, dense forest under a deep blue sky, the kind of sky that appears from time to time in the Midwest countryside.

The farmer turned from the black country road onto a gravel road that went into Stevens Point and onto a concrete bridge over the Wisconsin River, past a brick bakery.

The downtown was on the right, and bungalow houses on the left.

"Turn left, please. She's at 32 Second Avenue."

"It's a she? Oh dear, that spells trouble."

The farmer drove straight on a paved road past a row of pretty bungalow houses that nevertheless could use maintenance. They came to 32 Second Avenue, which was well maintained.

"Stop here, please."

The bungalow itself was painted yellow with brown trim, not too badly.

Cal got out. The farmer held out his hand. Cal shook it. The farmer shook Cal's hand away and held out his hand again.

"I never pay for my rides," Cal said and gently closed the door.

The farmer said something in a foreign language and drove off.

Cal took the black asphalt path between the yellow and brown bungalow house and the expansive green lawn of a park which was very pretty, with red and yellow autumn leaves. There was a jungle gym, a slide, and a sandbox. Saplings were shedding their golden leaves. There was a park bench facing a green wooden clubhouse with doors open. Cal sat on the bench.

Inside the clubhouse were three young people. A young woman in her early twenties was on the left. She had curly black hair and a maroon overshirt. A fat boy with a guitar strapped to his back was on the right. Against the back wall was Chris Carsten, wearing a thick yellow and white sweater with brass buttons, blue jeans, and loafers. She was not as blonde as she used to be, and she was also thinner. She was pasting cut-out motifs onto a piece of long green construction paper. She concentrated hard as she always did, sitting on the ground with her knees far apart. Cal tried not to look at her crotch.

After a while, Cal stood at the door. His shadow fell over Chris, and he said softly, "Chris Carsten."

She looked up. Her eyes widened. Her mouth opened, and her right hand went to cover her mouth.

"Cal Bedrick!" she said, then returned to her pasting.

The fat boy stood in front of him.

"What business do you have with Chris?" the fat boy said.

"We're old high school friends, aren't we, Chris?"

"I'm fat, but at least I work for a living. What do you do for a living? I bet you scrounge off other people. Your clothes are dirty," the fat boy said. He stood face to face, nose to nose with Cal "Don't ever hit a fat man. They've got all that mass behind them. They'll flatten you," he said.

"He's okay Eddie," Chris said, "you can sit down."

Eddie sat down and picked up his guitar but glared at Cal, who still stood in the doorway.

"My name is Eva Gorecki, Chris's housemate," the young woman in the maroon overshirt said.

"Polish?" Cal asked.

"Czech," Eva replied.

Chris handled a brush with white glue and deftly put the figures in place with long, slender fingers.

It went on that way for nearly an hour. A golden sun fell on Chris. They all yawned and stretched.

"That's enough for one day," Eva said.

They put their tools down and got up. Cal backed away. They locked the door from the outside.

Eddie went to a bench and sat, strumming his guitar. He sang "500 Miles."

Eva and Chris walked ahead side by side down the black asphalt path. The sun was further to the west and more red than orange. Cal followed a few steps behind, quite awkwardly.

"*I'll bet he's a masturbator*," Eva whispered.

Chris gently poked Eva in the side to keep her quiet.

They came around to the front of the yellow-brown bungalow and went up the creaking steps. Chris bent over to unlock the door.

Eva turned to Cal, who was still on the sidewalk. "Cal, we're having an early supper because we have to get up early tomorrow. Will you join us?"

"Bless you," Cal said.

"*What did you do that for?*" Chris mouthed to Eva.

"*I thought he was a friend of yours?*"

"*Are you kidding? He followed me all around. I couldn't get rid of him.*"

"*Oh well, he'll be gone soon.*"

"*You HOPE.*"

The door opened, and they all went in. The living room was average sized for a small bungalow, covered in a thin gray carpet nearly from wall to wall. Everything was clean. It smelled of mildew but was very nostalgic. A large fluffy gray cat jumped into Chris's arms.

A green vinyl easy chair was on the right, and a blue couch was on the left. Cal followed the girls into the kitchen. The kitchen floor was green, with splatterings of yellow.

"Sit down," Eva said.

Cal sat next to a small refrigerator by a window overlooking the red and yellow leaves of the saplings in the park.

The red and white oil cloth covered a small white wooden kitchen table. There was a small gas oven on which Eva sat a large spaghetti pot, half filled with water. She turned on the gas. Bubbles formed. Chris poured straight spaghetti strands into the bubbling pot. Eva stirred with a wooden spoon.

"Where's the men's room?" Cal asked.

Both girls pointed straight up without looking. Cal got up and walked to the stairwell by the blue couch. On the way back, he passed a tidy bedroom with a red, white, and blue quilt on a bed. There was a yellow nightgown on the bed and a black pebbled art portfolio against a wall. He went in, unzipped the portfolio, and looked at the paintings slowly, one by one.

They were mostly watercolors of pond shores and what grew there. Duckweed, autumn weeds hanging for life from little branches, a bit of duck fluff near a bit of algae, a sense of more water beyond a bank of river grass. The weather was uniformly bleak. They must have been painted on gray days. They were very sober, very detailed. There was a signature in the lower right corner, "*C. Carsten*".

He put the paintings back, zipped up the portfolio, and went downstairs. He sat by the refrigerator. Eva strained spaghetti in the sink and put three equal portions on three plates.

"Daumier has not had her supper," Eva said.

Chris got up. She poured cat food into a yellow plastic bowl that read "*Her Majesty*" in red letters. She put the bowl down in front of the closed back door.

Chris brought two plates to the table, and Eva brought the third and a jar of artichoke hearts which she put in front of Chris. Chris got a bowl of sauce and a soup spoon which she sat down in front of Cal.

"Tomato sauce, oregano, sage, black pepper, salt, and cumin. Sorry. No meatballs."

Eva put a plate down in front of Cal

"Help yourself."

Cal spooned some sauce on the spaghetti and began eating. The girls wound the spaghetti on a spoon while Cal used a fork and sucked it in, dropping strands on his trousers.

Eva went to the tap, wet a paper towel, and brought it to Cal, who stood and removed sauce from his trousers. He tried to remove the stain on his trousers without success. The stain only grew larger. He sat.

"Sorry," he said.

The girls paid no attention. Daumier was through with dinner. Eva opened the rear door and gently encouraged the cat to go out, which she did. She closed the door.

Eva slapped the table. "Forgot the wine," she said. She went to the counter and brought a bottle that held red Chianti. She poured it into their three glasses until the bottle was empty.

"That's it," Eva said.

"Finished," Chris said.

"Dead soldier," Cal said.

They looked at him.

"What does that mean?" Eva asked.

"It's army talk. Whenever you finish a bottle, you call it a dead soldier."

Eva put the empty bottle on the counter.

"Were you in the army, Cal?" she asked.

"No, but my father was. He was a master sergeant. He was well into his thirties when he joined. He was too old to have been drafted. He joined the Army Chemical Corps and was sent to Dugway Proving Grounds. While there, he noticed a chubby pianist who, like him, was a Jew. She played whatever you wanted, including Christian services. She had noticed him too. They both thought that the other had been taken, but that wasn't the case. When they found out, they took a stroll into the desert and came back engaged. He never told us what his chemical laboratory produced but he was about to be sent abroad to Europe when the war ended and the two of them were discharged. They got married off the post. He met her parents. She met his relatives. They went to Duluth, where he had been born and where he taught chemistry. After a couple of years, he got his PhD from the University of Wisconsin and then was hired by the University of Wisconsin extension center, a small outfit in an old brick building. He was strict. When I was thirteen, he was to give a lecture in Atlanta, but he never showed up. They sent a student to find out why and found him lying dead on his hotel bed. Cerebral hemorrhage. I went home, and that night, Dean Ahrnsbrock, the dean of the extension center, gave us the bad news about my father, taking his hat off under the yellow porch light full of moths. Sometimes at night, my father visits me when I am back in the Midwest."

There was a long silence.

"But you just said he was dead?" Eva said.

"He is."

There was another long pause.

"What about your mother?" Eva asked.

"She bled to death in California, so I heard."

There was another long pause.

Eva gently touched Cal's wrist. "Are you married, Cal?"

"No."

"Do you have a girlfriend?"

"No."

"Do you have a boyfriend?"

"No."

"Must be lonely."

They ate.

"Did you ever take art classes?" Eva asked.

"No. In seventh-grade art class, I forget the teacher's name."

"Crawford," Chris said without looking up from her spaghetti. "Mr. Crawford."

"I got a C on a painting," Cal said. "That's a low grade. I asked Mr. Crawford why. He pointed at it and said there's no subject. It's just trees, a road, and green grass. I felt then, and I feel now, that I had a perfect right to depict emptiness as I understood it. But I was a coward, and I painted a pale green 1949 Chevrolet with a round top. It was the car my mother owned. My father did not drive. Mr. Crawford gave me a B or B-minus."

"What other projects did you do?" Eva asked.

"Calligraphy."

"Oh wow, what did you calligraph?"

" 'American Imperialism is a Paper Tiger'."

"Wow, where did you get that from?"

"Mao."

"You were a leftie way back in seventh grade."

They ate.

"I heard you almost got married, Chris?" Cal said.

"Who told you?"

"Your mother."

Her mouth opened, and her eyebrows raised. "You talked to my mother about me?"

"Yes."

Chris grew moody. "Well, it never went through," she said.

"Why not?"

She leaned across the table towards Cal.

"Because he had a ..." she wrinkled her nose, "Jewish mother." Chris resumed her spaghetti. "I almost married someone I had known for exactly *one day!*" She crossed her eyes and shook her head.

"Do you have a boyfriend, Chris?"

Chris brightened. "Bob, he's a furniture designer. He's an excellent artist. He lives in a farmhouse in the country. That's where I'm going tomorrow morning."

"Would I like him?" Cal asked.

"Probably not."

"Why not?"

"He's very active," she laughed while looking at her plate. "Boy, does he like sex!"

There was a short pause.

"I'll take the plates and wash them," Eva said.

"Come with me, Cal. I'll show you my favorite part of the river," Chris said.

They got up. Chris took off her yellow and black sweater and put on a blue and gray sweater with round brass buttons.

"You wore that in high school."

"Did I?"

She went to the door, opened it, and went out. Cal joined Chris on the sidewalk. The sun had set. There were strange orange clouds far in the west.

"Have I changed much?" Chris asked.

"You look more Norwegian."

"I've lost weight."

"Are Scandinavians skinny?" Cal chuckled.

They went down a path and then off the beaten path to the river shore. The water was dark orange and dark blue. Eddies swirled on the far shore, which was studded with thin white and black birch trees. Two lads fished on the bank. One used a rod and reel, one used a bamboo pole. There were few rocks on the far side of the river. The currents of the river were either silver or green.

Chris sat on a boulder facing the river. Cal sat on a smaller boulder facing Chris. For a long time, they watched the water. Three trout swam past.

"Have you ever done cross-country skiing, Cal?" she asked.

"Nope."

"Well, I did, into the forest south of Thunder Bay. It was so quiet. It was like heaven. You should try it, Cal."

"Ok Chris, maybe I will."

There was a long pause.

"You never knew me, Cal," Chris said after a very long while.

A native boy gunned his motorboat, which carried five six-packs of Hamm's beer, downriver under the bridge by the brick bakery, and then went upstream. Large purple, gold, and white wakes spread from the bow. The noise of the motor subsided.

A tiny green and yellow leaf fell slowly onto Chris's light brown hair. Chris did not see the leaf or feel it. Cal bent towards her and reached across very slowly to pluck the leaf. Her head jerked back violently and to her left. Cal stopped still, then continued reaching. He pulled the leaf off her hair slowly and showed it to her. She made a face of apology. He dropped the leaf into the still water of the river just below his shoe.

The red, gold, and white wake from the native boy's motorboat pushed the leaf to shore. The sun had gone down across the far bank of the river.

Chris wrapped her sweater more tightly around herself. "It's getting cold and dark, let's go back in."

They walked back to the bungalow. It was dark inside except for the light over the stairwell so he could see his way to the bathroom.

"Come to bed, you two lovebirds. We're getting up early tomorrow," Eva called.

Chris went upstairs to her bedroom. Cal sat heavily on the blue couch, trying to make sense of things.

After a long while, Chris came out of her bedroom wearing the sheer yellow nightgown. She sat on the top step. She smiled. Cal stood from the couch and went up one step of the stairwell. After a long while, Cal took another step up towards her.

"I like your nightgown," he said.

She laughed cheerfully and hugged the nightgown around her knees. "Thanks. There's a hole in it," she said.

There was a pause. Cal went up one more step. She kept looking at him.

"Chris, I dreamed about you almost every morning for four years."

"I dreamed about you once, Cal. You came to me in my dream and said 'It will be alright Chris. Everything will turn out fine.' It was such a nice feeling."

That means you were having a hard time at Macalester for a while, Cal thought to himself.

Cal went up another step. She watched him.

Should I ask if I can sit on the same step as her?

"Cal, when do you start taking birth control pills?" Chris said.

Cal stopped. Now he was scared. Really and truly frightened. Who was this girl in front of him?

"I think I'll go for a walk," Cal said.

Chris looked at him, puzzled. He walked down the steps backward and walked out the door. Suddenly, Cal did not know where he was or who he was. Without warning, he was outside on the sidewalk, looking at the bungalow. He had not opened the door. Nobody had. The street side door was gone. There was no stairwell and no Chris. Wet autumn leaves soaked into his shoes.

"I better move on," he said nervously, "But where the hell am I?"

Cal walked away towards the bridge which he had crossed coming in. On his left was the brick bakery with lights on. It smelled fresh and wonderful. He held his head in both hands. The river was purple black with lots of small currents along the shores. He went down into the tall, wet grass. Many leopard-spotted frogs croaked, and lots of rough-skinned toads hopped around. He accidentally stepped into the river reeds.

Cal looked back at the bungalow house. The right and left walls of the house were crumbling slowly from the top down, and with equal slowness started leaning in towards each other, but they never reached one another.

Chris Carsten no longer concerns you. She has been buried in the park.

A terrible chill went through Cal, but he turned and made his way back to the bridge. His shoes squished all the way back to the yellow and brown bungalow and up the squeaky steps. He must have stepped on some living thing like a frog or a toad. He scraped his shoes on a step into the bungalow. He opened the door quietly and closed it equally quietly. It was entirely dark. He felt his way to the couch. He sat down shivering. He took off his wet shoes and socks and put them on the radiator. He tried to breathe deeply, but nothing came. He listened to the upstairs, but nothing moved. Should he take off his trousers which were soaked to the knees? After a very long time, he lay down on the blue couch. A blanket had been laid for him on the edge of the blue couch. He covered himself. He closed his eyes. He masturbated. He slept.

He heard the sound of Eva's alarm clock upstairs. He woke. He heard Chris brushing her teeth. He tried to sit, but he was groggy, very groggy. He needed both hands to hold himself upright on the couch. Chris came down the stairs, followed by Eva. Chris wore pale blue trousers and the same yellow and black sweater. She had a funny look on her face as if to say, "What were you up to last night?"

Eva came down the steps. Cal very carefully put on his wet socks and wet shoes, turned away, and put on his trousers which were now dry. They all went out the door. Eva locked it. Chris went to the Greyhound station to get a ride to Bob's farmhouse. Eva went to the A&P supermarket to replenish the groceries because she would be alone through the weekend. Cal went over the bridge past the bakery, which still had lights on and smelled terrific. He got to the gravel road that connected to the highway. He looked back. The eastern clouds were straight, flat, and ominous behind the park and the green wood clubhouse, which now seemed somewhat purple. The yellow-brown bungalow looked okay.

Once on the highway, Cal stuck out his right thumb. He hitched a ride in a very old VW Bug with a very old man. The old man had loose false teeth. Cal could hardly understand a word he said. As they drove along, the man kept muttering.

"Thish ish the teshting time."

It was nearing Halloween. On the left was an enormous pumpkin field. Men were severing their connections to the earth and loading them onto a large pickup truck.

A noisy and smelly turkey farm was nearby. Chaff and dust were being blown up by the wind. A man in a pale blue shirt with black suspenders, trousers, and rubber boots to his knees surveyed his fish farm.

"Such a load off my mind," Cal said.

"What?"

"I finished my unfinished business. I feel like a newborn atheist."

"I am a Jehovah'sh Witnesh."

The corn husks on both sides of the road were browned and curved down to the ground. Small pools of yellow and green algae turned at the shore to the right.

Cal dozed. The old man poked him. Cal woke. The old man pointed to the glorious grove of deciduous trees on the slope of Rib Mountain in between the evergreens leading up to the white rock formation known as Queen's Chair.

"I ushed to climb that," the old man said.

The old man turned and drove past bungalows and old suburban homes. He drove east towards the Wisconsin River. He came to the 3M factory.

"Stop here please. I know where I am," Cal said.

The battered old VW stopped. Cal opened the door and got out.

"May God bless you, sir," Cal said.

"It wash jusht an act of kindnesh."

Cal closed the door. The VW chugged away.

Chapter 3

Cal looked around. The swimming pool was wrecked. Grass filled the bottom. The depth markings at 3 feet, 6 feet, 8 feet, and 12 feet were still painted black on turquoise walls. The diving boards were gone.

It was at 3 feet where a playmate, Jack Monday, had yanked Cal's ankles out from under him when he was eight years old. Cal had fallen, screaming, face first into the water. He was rescued by one of the lifeguards. Jack Monday was hauled by the lifeguard, David Bernecke, to the boy's dressing room and undressed, which Jack Monday bitterly fought. When Bernecke pulled down Monday's bathing trunks the boy was wearing lady's pink panties. Bernecke cried out "pink panties" and all the other guys laughed. Jack Monday dressed instantly and ran out. Jack Monday had probably been expelled from school by then.

Between the adult pool and the Wisconsin River were the dressing rooms, with red brick bottom walls and white upper slats to let in sunlight and fresh air.

As for the Minnow pool, where toddlers pretended to swim while their parents watched from the stone seats of the amphitheater, these were gone, just grass, rock, and a hedge at the very top. There was no place to sit anywhere.

On the bank of the Wisconsin River were three aspens losing their leaves. Some fell into the river and began floating towards Stevens Point. Some fell on the black asphalt path leading to Duck Island.

A disconsolate man walked up the railroad tracks in a swarm of yellow butterflies. He sang:

If I had known when I was born
That butterflies would around me swarm
I would not have stirred in that hour or so
But waited for the coming of the Glory-O

Cal stepped carefully down the steep slope to the asphalt path leading to Duck Island. He walked along the river. A steep bluff dotted with trees, bushes, berries, and mushrooms was on his left, above was where he used to live. But he couldn't see the house now, and anyway he was too ashamed to let his family see him.

He walked to a familiar old white wooden bridge leading to a small island on the right side. He stopped. He patted the old white wooden bridge.

"Oh, father."

He tenderly crossed the bridge and lay down by the darkening water on the Stevens Point side. He took off his shoes. He closed his eyes and slapped at mosquitoes. He slept with his feet facing Stevens Point.

When he woke, a frog was sleeping on his chest. He nudged it off. The frog belched, plopped into the black, and swam to the old white wooden bridge behind Cal. It made it through the blackness into the algae to be with other frogs and turtles. Only his eyes and the top of his head were now visible. Cal giggled. Big Bull Falls roared to the north.

Cal went back to sleep. It was pitch black when he woke. No trees, no leaves, no nothing. He only saw his semi-transparent father slowly crossing the small island. His father had been dead for several years. He was 51. He had white crew-cut hair and wore a gray raincoat, gray trousers, and a red and gold tie. He was furious.

Cal sat up.

"Father, why are you transparent?"

"I'm dead. What are you doing here?"

"Yes, it's been four years. I've come back home, father. I am so happy to see you. Mom has gone back to college."

"Why did you take drugs?"

"I didn't."

"Do not lie to me Cal. That is one thing you must never do."

His father came closer.

"I tried something once or twice dad, but it was a nightmare. I'm glad to be home."

His father looked at him for a long time. "The rabbi told me you were goofing off when you should have been studying."

"I didn't goof off, dad. I would never do that, not in front of the rabbi anyway. He's boring."

His father paced the leaves in a circle.

"He escaped Germany through fields of dead men with their chests blown open. You don't know about such things. You're too young and egotistical."

There was a pause.

"I wanted you to be a great chemist, Cal."

"It was too hard," Cal said, "just too damn hard."

"Nothing is too hard. So you took drugs and went on the road, eh?"

"I'm sorry Dad, but I'm home now."

"You call this a home?"

His father walked away and disappeared.

Cal closed his eyes and tried to sleep.

"*Father*," he whispered.

When he woke, it was still dark. He was terribly hungry. He crossed the old white wooden bridge and went up the bluff. He kept going almost to the top of the bluff. It was muddy underfoot. A fat woman pushed a baby carriage. A feral dog loped down the main road. The fat woman rang a bell in the shape of an Austrian shepherdess. It rang musically.

Cal tried to eat mushrooms and berries but spat them out.

"Yuck! Yuck!"

He slid down the muddy path to the old white wooden bridge.

He found two duck eggs on the bridge. He cracked them open. They tasted awful. He dropped them into the black water, rushing by under the bridge going south. The eggshells bobbed, bounced, whirled, and after a long while, sank, half filled with water, on their way to Stevens Point but never getting there.

Cal leaned against a bridge post and fell asleep. When he woke, he saw the muddy white path leading back to the gray concrete bridge. He walked up the path. He could see plainly Big Bull Falls straight ahead to the north. To his left was a dapper young man in brown corduroy. He had a fresh haircut. Cal walked to the balustrade, a few feet away from the young man.

"If I smell bad, it's because I've been homeless for several nights. Please forgive me," Cal said.

"I forgive you," the dapper young man said. "But you must be terribly hungry?"

"I'm starving, sir."

"How long have you been down there?"

"Four or five nights."

"Dear Jesus, come with me, please." The young man took Cal's hand.

They walked together, hand in hand, over the algae pond down below. Cal watched frogs blinking in the algae. There were mud turtles below. Their scrawny reptilian snouts and eyes poked above the algae, hemmed in by fallen creosote-covered telephone poles that had rolled down from Harrison Boulevard at the top of a bluff. There were also one or two snapping turtles, each capable of taking your finger off, stalking flies.

There were sand turtles closer to the bluffs. They were small, light brown, and leathery. You couldn't catch them because as soon as you reached for them, there was a cloud of fine sand and a hole in the bank where the snout-nosed creatures had already burrowed in.

A cluster of black tadpoles wriggled ferociously, going nowhere in fairly still water. He looked up to the dry cleaners and saw a small pile of naphtha.

Chapter 4

Together, they crossed First Avenue at the top of the bluff, still holding hands. The fellow led him past two white propane tanks and quietly opened a glass-paneled door into a kitchen. A girl with red curly hair turned around and grinned. She was about twenty-two. Her gold cross flashed from her throat. She wore a white blouse, a white apron, and a long blue denim skirt.

"Oh, Charles, I'm just making breakfast. What have you got?"

"A homeless guy."

"Well, bring him in."

Cal stepped in.

"Homeless person, what's your name?"

"Cal Bedrick."

"Well, you are in the right place. My name is Frannie Sienkiewicz. We take care of the homeless here. Please sit at the table."

They both sat.

"I am starving. In fact, I think I might faint."

Frannie tossed five eggs into a black iron frying pan on the burner. They sizzled in the melting butter. She stirred them with a white rubber spatula.

"Oh my God, that smells so good," Cal said as his head dropped to the table. He fainted.

Charles dashed to keep Cal from falling to the floor. He made some coffee and put that in front of Cal.

"Drink, me hearty," Charles said.

Cal's eyes fluttered as he smelled the coffee. He opened his mouth. Charles put in a spoonful of coffee.

"Bless you Charles," Cal said.

"Charles, can you make two pieces of buttered toast for our guest?" Frannie said.

Charles got up, took out two slices of bread from a cold loaf in the fridge, and dropped them into the toaster. The toaster glowed red inside.

Frannie scooped the fried eggs onto a plate and placed it along with some cutlery in front of Cal, whose eyes began to blink. Charles gave him another spoonful of black coffee. Frannie put her right hand on Cal's back and slowly rubbed up and down. Cal began to faint again, but Frannie caught him over the eggs. Charles fed him spoonful after spoonful.

Cal began to cry.

"That's so good. God bless you all."

"Bless Jesus," Frannie said.

Charles fed him another spoonful of egg and put the toast into Cal's mouth. Cal chewed slowly and carefully.

"Good."

"Don't get your fingers near his mouth, Charles," Frannie warned.

Cal looked at Frannie hungrily. "By any chance, do you have any more eggs?"

Frannie laughed. She stood and cracked two more eggs on the sizzling pan of butter. They sizzled. She brought the fried eggs to Cal.

"Any toast?"

"My God, you are hungry."

"Yes, I've not eaten for a long time. I'm sorry for eating with my fingers, but I forgot how to eat any other way."

"It's okay. It's absolutely okay," Frannie said. "You look sleepy."

Cal bit into a buttered toast. "I am. I'm very sleepy. I haven't slept in nights."

Just then, a young boy, about eighteen, with sandy blonde hair and freckles, climbed down the stairs from what must have been the third floor landing into the kitchen and sleepily rubbed his eyes. He wore pajamas that ended in feet.

"Who's this guy?" he asked.

"His name is Cal. He'll stay with us tonight. He's homeless."

"Hi Cal, I'm Little Brother."

Little Brother sat at the dining table, pointed his eyes at the oil portrait, and said a quick prayer of gratitude to Jesus. Frannie served him coffee and scrambled eggs. Little Brother tucked into both with a fork.

Cal started to sleep in his chair.

"Let's put him in the living room," Charles said.

Charles picked Cal up by the armpits and walked him into a living room with black and white linoleum flooring and engravings of female saints on the walls. He gently laid Cal down on a red couch and wrapped him in a wool blanket.

Cal slept.

He woke later in the day. It was still light.

"Where am I?" he said.

Frannie was sitting on a chair by a brown oil heater, watching him.

"You may sleep as long as you like. That's what we're here for."

"I'm still a bit cold."

"Stay here."

Frannie went up the stairs and came back with two more wool blankets. She tucked them around Cal, who began to shiver.

"We'll have dinner in about two hours. I'll come and wake you."

Cal held onto her hand.

"Bless you," he said.

She smiled.

"Oh, Cal, your hand is so cold. Little Brother, could you go down into the basement and turn up the oil heater?"

"Right away, ma'am."

Little Brother opened a door behind Cal's head and went down into the basement. Flames roared from the black metal heater in the living room. Little Brother grinned, looked at Cal, and put his own rear end against the heater.

"Feels good," Little Brother said.

Cal smiled and closed his eyes. He went back to sleep.

In the early evening, the glass-paneled kitchen door opened. A tall, thin, freckled-faced fellow with brown hair tinged with red came in. He was around thirty.

"What are we having for dinner?" he asked.

"Lamb chops, Joey, your favorite," Frannie said.

"Do we have a new friend in the living room?"

"Yes, his name is Cal. He's homeless for now."

Joey sat down and prayed briefly to Jesus behind him.

"How did Cal find us?" Joey asked.

"Charles," Frannie said.

"I should have known."

After a while, light rain began to fall behind the Jesus portrait.

"Why don't we bring the homeless guy in for lamb chops," Joey said.

Little Brother and Frannie went to the living room to get Cal, who was already awake. They took him past a table with a statue of the Virgin Mary.

"What is that?" Cal asked.

"Our home altar."

They took Cal into the kitchen and sat him down at the dining table. Joey reached out and shook hands with Cal.

"I'm Joey."

"I'm Cal."

"Yes, I know."

"I'm very grateful to be here, and for breakfast from your wife and your brother."

"She's not my wife. She's my sister," Joey said.

"And anyway, I am the one who's going to marry her," Little Brother said.

Frannie blushed.

"Oh well, she's very cute anyway," Cal said.

Frannie grinned and served two freshly cooked plates of lamb chops to Joey, Little Brother, and Cal.

"Oh, how delicious," they all said in unison.

Little Brother picked up his piece using the thumb and forefinger of both his hands.

"Oh, Frannie, you're just wonderful," Little Brother said.

"I try to be, Little Brother."

Joey leaned over and cut Cal's lamb chop into six or seven pieces for him. Joey took a fork and put one piece in Cal's mouth.

"Bless you Joey," Cal said.

"Chew carefully," Joey said.

Frannie snapped her fingers. "Oh, the apple sauce," she said.

She went quickly to the refrigerator and brought out a bowl of apple sauce with a spoon. Cal dug in without sharing it. Frannie took the bowl from Cal, put a dollop on her own plate, put a bit on Little Brother's plate, and then gave the bowl to Joey.

"Are you heating bread?" Joey asked.

Frannie slapped herself on the forehead.

"Gosh, I can't remember anything today."

She went to the stove and put on an oven mitt. She pulled out hot bread rolls and put them in a wicker basket. She put them on the table with a small tub of butter.

"Come on, guys, I can't have forgotten anything else," Frannie said.

They could hear pitter-patter on the roof and ceiling.

"I got home just in time, didn't I?" Joey said.

Little Brother leaned over and kissed Frannie on the cheek. A big, boisterous kiss.

"Thank you for another wonderful dinner, Frannie. Cal, do you have blankets in the living room?"

"I do."

"Shall we walk you back?" Little Brother asked.

"I would appreciate that very much."

Frannie stood up, put an arm around Cal's waist, and walked him past the home altar. She lay him down on the three blankets on the red couch. She tucked him in and gently pinched his cheek.

"Are you warm enough?" she asked.

"Warmer, thank you."

"Well, I'm upstairs in my bedroom. If you get cold, just gently call my name."

Cal reached for her hand but missed. Frannie went upstairs.

Outside it was dark, and the windows looking out onto the Third Avenue entrance glimmered from passing traffic.

Cal fell asleep.

Chapter 5

The following day Frannie was awake early and carving pumpkins at the sink. It was the day before Halloween.

Cal got up slowly, and limped into the kitchen.

"Can I help?" he asked.

"That's very kind of you, Cal," Frannie said. She pointed at a cutlery drawer to the right side of the sink.

"Please get me a short sharp knife," she said. "It's in the drawer on your left."

Cal did so. There were three pumpkins on Frannie's side. One of them had been carved at the top. Cal took the two that had not been carved and sliced the tops off. He kept blinking.

"Are you alright Cal?"

"Fit as a proverbial fiddle. Where's Joey?"

"He's at work."

"What about Charles?"

"Only Jesus knows."

They both carved for a long time without saying anything, from time to time tossing bits of pumpkin into the waste basket below the sink.

"Is Charles your boyfriend?"

There was a long pause.

"Nope, he's not," Frannie laughed after a long while.

"You know Frannie, my father died when I was thirteen. My mother became depressed, and I learned how to cook. I can make pumpkin soup and pumpkin pie if you'd like?"

"Can you? That would be absolutely wonderful Cal."

Little Brother came down the stairs yawning as usual.

"Can I have some money mom? I've got to get some goodies at the Piggly Wiggly and the drug store. They should be open by now."

Frannie reached into her purse, which was on the kitchen table. She gave Little Brother twenty dollars.

"Don't forget the long white dinner candles. We'll put them inside the pumpkins to show people we mean business."

Little Brother skipped out of the kitchen door and up Stuart Avenue, turning left onto Third Avenue. He crossed into the Piggly Wiggly and waved to Joey, who was busy stocking fish on ice. Joey grinned. Little Brother took three handfuls of candies, including caramels, and put them in three light brown paper bags.

"Can you please weigh these three bags of Halloween goodies and charge them all to Joey?" he said to Edna, the cashier.

"He's not the manager yet," she said.

"Well, he will be. It's only a matter of days."

Wilkins, a native man, came into the store carrying bags of venison and fish. They had special rights to hunt and fish. He put them on Mr. Zimbauer's desk. Mr. Zimbauer paid him. He nodded, hugged Mr. Zimbauer, and left the store. Little Brother waved to Mr. Zimbauer, and then crossed to the drug store where the pharmacist was already at the counter at the rear of the store, waving and smiling. Two high school kids were having malted milks at the front counter. There was a portrait of the homecoming queen Vicki Aubourg and a picture of coach Win Brockmeyer. Below was a color photo of the stars drafted by the Los Angeles Rams, "Crazy Legs" Hirsch and Jim Oakland.

On the side were two protruding iron racks. One held "Go Lumberjacks" T-shirts featuring Bucky Badger, who had tough fists ready to strike. Wisconsin was called The Badger State because in the nineteenth century tin miners dug deep holes into the earth in the north part of the state, so it looked like badgers had been there.

The next rack sold sweatshirts, all white except for large red and white stenciled *W*'s.

Little Brother scooped up five brown bags filled with hard candies, caramel, and licorice. He paid for them at the malted milk counter, waved to the pharmacist, and left.

Little Brother turned the corner and went to Stuart Avenue and then walked down the abnormally long lawn leading straight to the kitchen door of the Sienkiewicz home. He took the candies to the living room and put them on a wicker basket resting on a green and beige card table.

Cal took the carved pumpkins and put them out in front of the Third Avenue door and the kitchen door.

"What's this?" Cal asked, pointing to a round marble slab resting on a round wood holder in the living room corner. "A liquor cabinet?"

"No, we don't drink hard liquor, only Polish beer. We keep our Christmas ornaments in there."

Cal looked out the windows behind the oil heater. Pumpkins were already set up across the street. Houses were decorated with white soap skeletons and witches on brooms, just like Third Avenue.

The glass-paneled kitchen door opened. Joey came in, sweating.

"Rough day, boss?" Frannie asked.

"Oh yeah, you could say that."

"Well, have some candies. They're in the living room."

"Don't mind if I do."

The next day was October 31, Halloween night. Shadows fell from the west side of Third Avenue. Frannie lighted candles and placed them in the pumpkins at the Third Avenue door and outside the kitchen door. Kids were already in costumes and holding bags for treats. The sun was down in the west. Frannie stepped outside the Third Avenue door to await her first trick-or-treater, a three-year-old toddler holding her father's hand. She wore round red plastic shoes and big black mouse ears.

"Are you Minnie or Mickey?" Frannie asked.

She looked up at her father and whispered, "*Dad, am I Minnie or Mickey?*"

"You're Minnie, darling."

The toddler turned to Frannie and smiled, "I'm Minnie, darling!"

"What do you say before I give you candies?"

The toddler frowned. She whispered to her dad, "*Daddy, what do I say?*"

"*Trick or treat,*" he whispered.

She turned to Frannie with bright eyes, smiling eagerly. "Twick-o-tweet," the girl said.

Frannie gave her a little package of M&M's. She pointed to the M's. "See, M for Mickey, M for Minnie." She dropped it into the toddler's bag.

"Look what I got! Look what I got!" the toddler said as she walked away, waving her bag.

Little Brother turned off the exterior light and turned on the living room light.

It was dark. A witch came by, two green goblins, and a boy in a winter coat with a towel where his head should have been so that he looked headless.

"I'm a headless horseman," he said.

Frannie picked up the pumpkin by the door and put it right where the kid's head looked like it should be.

"Wow, thank you," the kid said.

Little Brother put three miniature Tootsie Rolls in his bag.

The kid walked away and turned to wave. Wouldn't you know it, the pumpkin fell and splintered all over the sidewalk and onto Third Avenue. The boy shrugged. Little Brother and Frannie chuckled, shrugged, waved, and went in.

After a while, there was another knock at the door. This time Cal got up. A young boy around seven years old, wearing a Mighty Mouse costume, said "Trick or treat, sir," as he held his mother's hand.

Cal reached for several caramels and put them quickly into the boy's bag.

"Thank you, sir," the boy said.

"You're more than welcome."

Cal closed the door and went back to the card table where he nibbled on a caramel. Frannie playfully slapped his hand. It was especially dark outside now on both sides of Third Avenue.

There was another knock at the door. Frannie went out. It was an adolescent with army fatigues and a plastic BB rifle.

"Who are you?" Frannie asked.

"Charlie Starkweather."

Next to him stood a girl.

"Who are you?"

"I'm his fourteen-year-old girlfriend."

"Don't you think you're a bit old for Halloween?"

"I'll shoot you if you don't give me candy," the boy said.

Little Brother came out. "What's going on?" he asked.

"Nothing," Frannie replied.

The Charlie character pointed his plastic rifle at Frannie.

"Please do me a favor and go away," Frannie said.

The boy aimed the rifle at Little Brother's genitals.

"LARRY!" Frannie shouted.

Little Brother turned sideways. Two BBs hit him in the hip.

"Didn't feel a thing, asshole," Little Brother said, grabbing the BB gun from Charlie.

Meanwhile, the fourteen-year-old girl pushed Frannie, who fell on her rump. Frannie laughed and winced as she got up and dusted her rear end off.

"Haven't fallen there since I was five."

Frannie approached the girlfriend very casually. They both smiled at each other. Suddenly Frannie pushed her hard onto her rump.

"Ow!" she said. "Charlie, pick me up."

Charlie was busy with Little Brother, who had wrestled the BB gun out of the boy's arms. Little Brother went quickly to the sidewalk grate. He emptied the BB chamber completely and then threw the BB gun into the middle of Third Avenue, where it was run over by a moving van.

"Hey!" Charlie yelled.

The moving van ran over the rest of the BB gun, which was now useless. Little Brother stepped up to Charlie.

"Get back to the Hollow, or I will flatten you right here and now."

Charlie took a step backward.

"You wouldn't dare."

Little Brother took a step forward.

"Try me."

"Charlie, get me up," the girlfriend said.

"She's calling for your help. Don't just stand there," Little Brother said.

Charlie pulled the girl up. They both walked quickly backward. Charlie pointed to Little Brother.

"Somebody ought to kill you."

"Well, it ain't you, that's for sure."

"Little Brother, should I get the rifle?" Frannie asked.

"No, these guys are jerks."

He took two steps forward. They took four steps backward, turned, and started galloping toward the Hollow on the far side of Third Avenue.

"Let's go in. I'm hungry," Little Brother said.

It was quiet at the candy bowl. Joey came in through the kitchen door with a Lone Ranger mask on. He put a hand on Cal's shoulder.

"Boo!"

"Oh Joey, don't scare us," Frannie said.

"We sold two tons' worth of caramel at the Piggly Wiggly. All of Third Avenue is decorated with soap drawings. You should see it!"

"I did! Look at some of the stuff I bought," Little Brother said.

Joey sat down in front of the Third Avenue window. He handed Frannie a deluxe box of Piggly Wiggly fudge.

"What in the world am I going to do with this, Joey?"

"Put it in the kitchen cabinet. We'll keep it for Thanksgiving."

Frannie got up and put the fudge in the kitchen cabinet. She came back holding a bowl of Cal's pumpkin soup with spoons in it.

"Good Lord, who made this?" Joey asked.

"You won't believe it. It was Cal. He also made a pumpkin pie!"

"We better keep the guy," Joey said.

They ate.

"Whatever happened to Charlie Starkweather?" Frannie asked.

Joey looked up, startled. "Electrocuted in Nebraska," he said.

"What happened to his girlfriend?"

"She was sent to Nebraska State Prison for Women. She was too young to be electrocuted," Cal said.

"How many people did he kill?" Frannie asked.

"Eleven," Cal replied.

"Why the sudden interest in the mass killer?" Joey asked.

"Because a punk kid pretending to be Charlie Starkweather tried to hold me up with a BB gun demanding candies."

Joey stood up. "Where are they now?" He opened the door. "Which way did they go?"

"Relax, big brother, they're long gone by now. I think they live in the Hollow."

There was a silence. Joey came back in and sat back down. He unwrapped a caramel and chewed it.

"Wha' happened," he asked with his mouth full.

"I punched the rifle out of Charlie's hands and threw the BB gun onto Third Avenue. It got run over by a moving van. It's completely useless, I promise you," Little Brother said.

Joey nodded, "They'll never resurface. Well done, Little Brother."

Joey stretched luxuriously, making big fists with his powerful hands. He had been on the basketball team, which, to everyone's surprise, had won the state high school basketball championship, beating the tall, lanky players from Milwaukee but also the shorter yet infinitely tough farm boys from Dodge.

"Tomorrow is a special day," he said.

"Yes, All Saints' Day," Frannie said.

"Yes, but also, JOEY SIENKIEWICZ'S FIRST DAY AS MANAGER OF WAUSAU'S THIRD AVENUE PIGGLY WIGGLY!"

He took keys out of his pocket and rattled them over his head in triumph. They all applauded. Joey bowed.

"Thank you, my children," he said.

They all continued slurping Cal's pumpkin soup.

"This soup is terrific, Cal. I should hire you." Joey said.

Cal grinned. "Well, maybe. I am looking for work."

"You're always on the go, aren't you?" Joey chuckled.

"I'll work hard Joey, I promise."

Frannie raised her eyebrows.

"You could use the help from a new stock boy when you're managing the Piggly Wiggly. I'd take that offer if I were you, Joey."

"I have to think about it," Joey said.

They finished their soup.

Just then, seven somnambulists in black sheets with eyeholes passed by outside the darkened street behind Joey.

"Who are they?" Cal asked.

Joey stood up, went to the front door, opened it, and stepped out.

"Excuse me, my friends, who are you? Are you a religious sect?"

The group paused. "No, we are not a religious group. We are somnambulists, a cult of like-minded persons of the town who wish to sleepwalk through the dark and terrible times. But we mean no harm to you or your family, sir," one of the members said.

Joey, slightly flustered, bowed and then went back into the house.

"Well, who were they?" Cal asked.

"Somnambulists."

"What are they?" Little Brother asked.

"They're not a religious sect, just a cult."

"Are they dangerous?"

"Nope, they just sleepwalk through life. Many people are like that."

The Sienkiewiczes ate leftover candies. Cal had his fair share.

On the other side of Third Avenue some more grown-up kids were accompanied by their parents.

Headlights glinted on light rain. Tires made rubbery noises on the wet pavement and splashed up to the hub caps. Across the street there was a row of bungalow houses, each with lighted jack-o'-lanterns, luminous skeletons, or witches with beady eyes. Streetlights came on.

Further away downstream, the Wausau Hotel and Bar glowed eerily. Yellow-orange lights spilled out onto the side road, the grassy hill, and across the river. Gap-tooth lighted jack-o'-lanterns gleamed on the windowsills. Interlocked chains of black and orange crepe paper dangled from the ceiling. The Wausau Hotel and Bar was very crowded; the music inside was rhythm and blues.

The bartender had concocted a special brew called Witches' Brew. It was a combination of Jamaican rum, brandy, beer, and gin. It was deadly, but popular.

A woman in a long blue dress with ruffles at the bottom stumbled out between two giant symmetrical pumpkins flanking the front door, stepped onto the lawn facing Stevens Point, leaned over, and threw up.

The green grass down to the riverfront sparkled. On the west side of the river, bright orange liquid discharged from the 3M plant, floated into the black water and slowly sank. Motorboats with music coming from them chugged toward Stevens Point.

Chapter 6

It was November 1, All Saints' Day. Frannie and Little Brother went down to the Christian cemetery, which was very foggy. Christian shadows moved vaguely under the pine trees.

"No, it's this way, Little Brother," Frannie said.

They found the highly polished red granite Sienkiewicz tombstone. It was an obelisk. Frannie put a red votive candle on its base. She lighted the candle. It joined the other red lights guttering on other tombstones throughout the cemetery. They prayed.

Jacek "Jack" Sienkiewicz
A Loving Husband and Father, and a Brave Soldier.
Born in Poznan, Poland
Died in Wausau, Wisconsin

The tomb had a white cross embedded in it. Below the cross, it read:

Anna Magdalena Sienkiewicz
Beloved Mother of Three. A Blessing to Us All
Born in Lodz, Poland
Died in Wausau, Wisconsin

They stood and crossed themselves, then held hands in a moment of silence. They turned to leave. Frannie tripped over a shrouded evergreen bush. Little Brother caught her and guided her to the cemetery gates.

"Can we look at Daddy's war album now?"

"Yes of course, Little Brother."

A light rain was sprinkling down. Frannie wiped her cheeks. They walked back to the Jesus house, went upstairs toward Frannie's bathroom, and turned right into what would have been their mother and father's bedroom. Frannie pulled out a well-worn red leather photo album from a shelf. She sat down and opened the first page.

It showed their father, quite young, dressed in Polish army fatigues. He wore a pistol in his belt. It was a captured German Luger. She turned the pages. There was a picture of their father at a camouflaged cannon. It was nearly covered in surrounding foliage. A machine gun rested on top of the cannon. Two or three Polish soldiers grinned for the camera.

"Who won the war?" Little Brother asked.

"The Germans invaded from the south and the Russians invaded from the east."

"What happened to Poland?"

"Disappeared. But we had friends in America and in England who beat both the Germans and the Russians."

"Is that why we came to America?"

"Pretty much."

"Will Russia and Germany invade America?"

Frannie tussled Little Brothers hair. "Unlikely, Little Brother, very unlikely."

There was a photo of their parents' wedding at Our Lady of the Holy Sepulcher. Their father had excellent posture, his shoulders back. It had been a nuptial wedding, which meant that vows were exchanged during the mass. Somebody had taken a picture of Jack putting the ring on Anna's ring finger. He was saying something, probably "With this ring, I thee wed." They were both smiling a lot.

The next photo showed the building of the Jesus house with Jack and his Polish friends. There was already a flowerbed on the Duck Island side and an improbably long lawn on the Stuart Avenue side.

"See, it doesn't look like the other houses on the block because our father didn't follow the normal pattern," Frannie said.

"Yeah, our house is so much bigger than the others," Little Brother said.

There was a photo of little Joey standing in the doorway of what was now Frannie's bedroom. He looked puzzled, but he was grinning. The final picture was of Little Brother.

"That's me," Little Brother said.

He stared at the photo for a long time and finally closed the photo album. He handed it back to Frannie, who put it in its place on the shelf.

"Mommy, can you and I get married?"

"No honey, you're my brother. We can't get married."

"You're wrong. I know it."

They walked out of their parents' room.

"You know, Mommy, we had such a handsome, brave father. A real soldier," Little Brother said as they went down the stairs.

Chapter 7

The next morning, Frannie made breakfast. Cal ate. When he was through, he banged the table politely and stood.

"Thanks for a wonderful breakfast, Frannie. I'm going to visit the folks. I don't know how long this will take, but I should be back soon."

Frannie squeezed Cal's cheek. He leaned forward to kiss her, but she backed off. He went out the door and onto First Avenue, which used to be Harrison Boulevard. He began walking west across from trees and foliage across the park side. He walked past red and white bungalows and blue and green bungalows. He came to the bungalow of his old friend Leroy Clark, who was probably no longer living there.

One day, years ago, Leroy hit a seven-year-old girl in the countryside on his new motorcycle. It was a sickening collision. Leroy somersaulted over the front handles. He landed on his feet in front of the unconscious girl.

"Oh no, no," Leroy said.

Traffic began to slow as Leroy waved his arms. An ambulance eventually arrived at the scene. It took almost an hour to get the two to Memorial Hospital.

Leroy came to school with a brace. Within the week, a uniformed policeman knocked on the glass pane of Mrs. McGill's trigonometry class. It got completely quiet. Leroy had a hunch about what had happened to the girl, and so did everybody else. He sat up very, very slowly. Everybody in the class looked at the policeman. Leroy took a long time straightening out his pencils and worksheets. He finally came to the door, went outside and closed the door behind him. Still, everybody heard the policeman say, "The girl died." Leroy fainted, blond duck-ass haircut and all.

Cal kept walking up to the corner. A badger crawled out of a hedge. Cal carefully avoided it. They're dangerous and carnivorous. The sun was going down. It was golden in the west. Cal went by the front door of his old house, which had been a two-family clapboard house. Nobody seemed to be inside. He walked around the corner block past a huge American flag, which he had never seen the likes of before. He turned down West Boulevard. There were no flowers at the basement side of the house anymore, only rolled-up turf seeded with grass. Nobody had bothered to plant those yet. He kept walking past an old telephone pole and then turned to an old wooden clapboard garage at the rear of the house. There was a small sign on the glass of the garage. Cal went up to read it.

If you're close enough to read this, you're in range

The backyard no longer had lilac trees, but it still had a rusted cylindrical burner in the very center of the rough grass. Cal went over and touched the burner. It was still warm. He walked up the steps to what had been his back door and knocked at the glass doorway. Nobody answered. It was dark inside. He went down the steps.

The driveway was no longer pink gravel but black asphalt, and there were no lilies of the valley at the basement door and no coal chute. Cal wiped his eyes and went back to take a nap by the old burner. He snoozed, snoring gently. Gentle silver raindrops fell on his face and sparkled. After a while, he heard the clop of heavy shoes coming up the other stairs. He turned over on his side. A man carrying two heavy bags from the Piggly Wiggly clumped up the steps.

"Get off my property!" he yelled.

Cal woke up warily. Rain began to fall.

"This used to be our property."

"Well, it's not now, is it? I'm not going to warn you again. Cross the road and get outta here."

Cal stood up and went groggily to the far side of the driveway. The man followed.

"Hurry up and move your ass!"

Cal twitched his rear end and, without turning, flipped him the bird. The man went inside. Cal jumped on the porch. After a while, the door re-opened. The man clomped his way to Cal and kicked him in the ribs.

"I said GET OUT! What's the matter with you?"

"It's raining, asshole."

"That does it." The man said. He went back inside and peeked out. "Would the gentleman prefer a shotgun or a pistol?"

Cal didn't respond. The man came out with a pistol and fired twice at Cal. Cal jumped off the porch into a hard, hard rain. The man followed.

"Jesus Christ!"

Cal hid behind the flagpole. The man shot at Cal again. Cal dodged left. Cal dodged right. Just then, a moving van with bright headlights turned the corner of First Avenue and stopped. The driver turned on the overhead lights to look at a city map.

The lights disoriented the shooter, who covered his eyes. Cal charged forward, reaching for the pistol, and bending it out of the shooter's hand.

"My wrist! You fucker! You've crippled me!"

"Well, you damn near killed me, asshole!"

Lightning was cracking along the road. The van driver turned off the headlights and continued forward. Cal took the gun, emptied the chamber, and threw it as far as he could, high and wide, deep into the bushes. They both ran across the road.

"I'm getting my shotgun, asshole!" the man yelled.

"Well, you know where to stick it!"

Cal quickly walked toward Stuart Avenue, trying to find the Jesus house. It was absolutely black outside, and thunder was crashing. He hid for a while in the bushes of Leroy Clark's old bungalow and then ran fast toward Stuart Avenue. He recognized the two propane tanks from the Jesus house. He ran to the kitchen door and knocked hard. Frannie opened the door. He was dripping everywhere. She stared at him.

"What the hell has happened to you? You're all wet. You must be starving. For God's sake, sit down and eat."

"T . . . th . . . thank you."

Little Brother ran upstairs and got several bath towels. He draped them over Cal.

"What happened to you, Cal? It's raining like hell out there. It's the worst storm I've ever seen," Joey said.

"I was shot at by a guy who lived in the clapboard house that I grew up in. I ran across the street. He chased me. Luckily, he was blinded by the brights of a moving van. I grabbed his right wrist and twisted it damn near off. I got hold of his pistol and threw it as hard and as far as I could down the bluff. I couldn't tell where it landed."

"We'll go find it tomorrow and shoot the daylights out of that guy," Little Brother said.

Frannie crossed herself.

"No, you won't. We will not have violence coming from the Jesus house, and Cal needs to sleep and rest. Tomorrow we will report what happened to the police."

Just then, a huge crack of lightning hit First Avenue. Everybody winced.

"I'll bet the lodge on Duck Island is burning," Little Brother said.

Another bolt of lightning cracked overhead as Frannie put lamb chops on a plate. She put the plate in front of Cal along with a knife and fork and a glass of milk. She rubbed Cal's back.

"God, I hope it doesn't hit the roof," Joey said.

They all prayed to Jesus.

"Jesus, we are very mindful of our storm, but please save our house."

Joey buttered a roll of bread that was still warm and crisp. He put it on Cal's plate. Cal wolfed it down.

"B . . . b . . . bless you, bless you all and bless Jesus."

"Let's put him to bed before he gets pneumonia," Joey said.

Cal stood. Frannie walked him past the home altar into the living room and lay him down on the red couch.

Rain was pounding at the Third Avenue door and at the pantry door. Frannie came down with an armful of warm towels.

She lay them on Cal. She turned on a light by the home altar and another by the Third Avenue door. She sat by the oil heater. Cal's teeth chattered. He slept, snoring lightly.

When he woke, it was at least 3 AM and very dark. The rain had stopped. He heard somebody trying to unlock the Third Avenue door.

"Little Brother! Little Brother! Wake up! Somebody is trying to break in."

Little Brother rushed downstairs and grabbed the rifle from the pantry. He hid behind the brown metal oil burner in the living room and aimed at the opening doorway.

"Let him come in. I'll blow off his head," he said.

There was a loud bang.

"Frannie!" Cal yelled.

Frannie ran down to Cal and cradled him. He was bleeding from his forehead. She called the police.

Joey ran down from his third floor bedroom.

"What just happened?" Joey said.

"He's been hit in the face by buckshot. Get some warm water, a bowl, and some tweezers. I'm waiting for the police to show up."

Joey began plucking buckshot out of Cal's forehead with tweezers and dropping them in the bowl where they clinked into the water.

A police car pulled up.

"They're here," Little Brother said.

Joey grabbed the rifle from Little Brother and went around the corner of the house to the long lawn. The man crawled towards the kitchen cradling a shotgun. Joey put down his rifle and pointed. "Over there, he's over there."

Two officers jumped out of the front seat brandishing black revolvers. They shot at the intruder but missed.

The intruder swiveled and shot at the officers but he too missed although they heard the metal pieces clunk against the patrol car.

The two officers stepped quickly but gingerly until they were standing right over the intruder, who had trouble handling his shotgun. They put their revolvers against the side of his head and pulled the trigger three times. "Is he dead?" Little Brother asked from the kitchen.

"You better believe it," a cop said.

Joey shuffled carefully, but very visibly, holding out Emma, the rifle, to the cops.

"I am Joey Sienkiewicz. The manager of the Piggly Wiggly. I live here along with my younger sister, younger brother, and a homeless person we are taking care of."

One of the cops went inside.

"Cal here got hit with buckshot from a shotgun. He's in poor shape," Joey said, following the cop into the house.

The cop kneeled on the stairs and examined Cal's forehead wounds. He gently turned Cal over.

"He's hurt bad, isn't he? He should go to the hospital."

"No, no hospital for me," Cal said.

"You're bleeding very badly, sir."

"Then I'll bleed. Just let me bleed. I'll clean it up in the morning."

"I can't promise you'll have a morning if you don't go to the hospital. Are you in pain?"

"I've had worse."

A second patrol car pulled up outside. Neighbors had gathered around the Sienkiewicz home on the sidewalk and on Stuart Avenue. Newspaper photographers were flashing their cameras at the spot where the intruder had died. Some guys were looking in from the Third Avenue doorway where the intruder's blood was still bright red.

Chapter 8

The next morning Cal stood at the stove. He had bandages over his forehead and one of his eyes. He wore a white apron. When Joey came down the stairs it was still dark.

"What would you like for breakfast, boss?" Cal said.

"What can you cook?" Joey said, surprised.

"Whatever you want sir, I can make anything. French toast, scrambled eggs, anything you like, you tell me. My father died when I was thirteen, my mother became depressed, and I became the family cook."

Confused, Joey went to his seat under the oil portrait of Jesus and prayed in gratitude for the food he was about to eat.

"Two pieces of French toast would be lovely and some coffee with milk. Thank you."

Cal got butter frying in a black iron pan on the stove. He used the drip percolator, and then dropped bread into the black iron pan, which was already sizzling with butter.

Cal looked out the kitchen window. "At least it's not raining today," he said.

"Don't be so sure. Sometimes it snows later on. After all, it's November, isn't it?" Joey said.

Cal put two slices of French toast on a plate and put it in front of Joey along with a bottle of Aunt Jemima syrup. He went to the cutlery drawer and put a knife and fork to the side of the plate.

"Dig in, boss," Cal said.

Joey took a tentative slice, closed his eyes, and nodded vigorously. "It's good, Cal. Delicious."

Cal sat down at the table, pleased.

"Would you hire me?" Cal said.

"As cook?"

"Maybe as your assistant at the Piggly Wiggly. I really need some money, Joey. I need to buy new clothes. I can't go around town like this."

Joey mumbled with his mouth full, "Come with me tomorrow morning."

Cal smiled broadly.

Frannie came down the steps sleepily.

"I heard talking. What's going on? Have you any idea what time it is?"

"Hi Frannie, do you like my apron?"

"It's beautiful."

"I couldn't find your French chef's hat."

"My gosh," she said, "I'm supposed to serve you."

"Sit down. What would you like for breakfast? You can have anything you want."

"Really?"

"Absolutely."

Frannie thought for a while, then grinned the Sienkiewicz grin.

"I would like two pears in pear juice."

"Coffee?"

"Black. Thank you."

Cal reached into the fridge, got out a can of pear halves, found a can opener, and with a spoon, put two pear halves in a bowl and took it along with black coffee to Frannie. She widened her eyes.

"Oh yum. What about a napkin?" she asked.

"If mademoiselle wishes a napkin, mademoiselle shall have a napkin."

Cal reached behind him and plucked out a napkin from near the toaster.

He lay a hand on her right shoulder. She tucked into one of the pear halves, closed her eyes, and nodded.

"Thank you, this is wonderful."

Little Brother came down the steps in his flannel pajamas that were printed with drawings of yawning moose.

“What would you like for breakfast, Little Brother?” Cal asked.

“Two slices of toast with peanut butter and marmalade, and a fruit juice.”

“Okay, but have you prayed?”

“Forgot.”

“Well, get busy.”

Little Brother turned to the portrait of Jesus, folded his hands, and mumbled thanks for breakfast. Cal served toast with peanut butter and marmalade and a cup of sweet apple juice. Frannie leaned back and sipped up the pear juice.

“What a treat,” Frannie said as she stood. “I might as well wash the dishes.”

“You wash, I’ll dry,” Cal said.

Frannie giggled.

“What’s going on here, Cal?”

“I’m happy to be alive.”

Frannie brought the dishes and bowls and put them on the left side of the sink. She took a sponge, soaped the cutlery, then handed it to Cal, who rinsed and dried it on his white apron. Cal put the dry cutlery in a blue rubber dish rack. He sipped a bit more of the coffee. Frannie soaped another dish and handed it to Cal.

“Come on, you lazy bum, I’m way ahead of you,” Frannie said.

Cal took it and rinsed it, then dried it on his apron and put it in the rubber dish rack.

“Joey, it’s getting on in time,” Frannie said.

Joey looked up at the clock.

“Oh my God!” Joey said.

He jumped up from his chair and put on his red and white basketball jacket.

“Oh, he’s got on his lucky basketball jacket. This will be interesting.” Frannie said.

“Go, champ, go!” Little Brother said.

Joey dashed out the door, closing it hard, and scooted up Stuart Avenue. Frannie handed Cal coffee cups.

“I was waiting for these,” Cal said.

“Well, stop complaining. You’ve got them.”

This time, when Cal dried the cups and put them in the blue rubber dish rack, he stopped to look out the window.

"Oh! An owl!"

"Where?" Frannie said.

"Right there over First Avenue. Can't you see it?"

Frannie peeped out of the window. "No."

Cal took his left arm, put it around Frannie's left shoulder, and then pulled her to his side of the sink. She leaned against him comfortably.

"Oh, there he is! Hi Mr. Owl!" she said.

The kitchen door opened. Cal let go of Frannie.

"Am I too early or too late?" Charles said.

"Depends on your point of view," Cal said. "I'm the cook this morning. What would you like?"

"Scrambled eggs?"

"Pray first," Cal said.

Frannie smiled and put a piece of toast with butter in front of Charles along with scrambled eggs. Cal went back to the owl.

"That's the same owl I saw on my first day at Duck Island," Cal said.

"Wowie zowie," Charles said.

"Let's go out and take a look at the guy," Frannie said, putting the last dried cup in the blue rubber dish rack.

"I haven't had my breakfast yet," Charles mumbled.

"Now, Mr. Szymanski, let's get a move on," Frannie said, wiping her hands on a kitchen towel.

Charles stood, took up a piece of scrambled egg in his hand, and put it in his mouth. Frannie put on her fake fur winter coat. Cal put on one of Little Brother's heavier jackets and motioned to Charles to join them. They all went out of the kitchen, letting the door swing shut.

They all walked up First Avenue and stopped under the owl, which was sitting on a bare branch watching them.

"Hi Mr. Owl," Charles said.

The owl looked straight down at the trio.

"Where were you standing when you threw the dead man's revolver into the bluff?" Little Brother asked.

Cal began walking quickly.

"I'll show you!"

They all trotted quickly on the dirt path under the leaves.

"Where was he standing?" Little Brother asked.

Cal stood at the corner of First Avenue.

"Right here."

"In the middle of the intersection?" Little Brother asked.

"Yup."

"And where were you?"

"I was still on the path. A truck driver turned the corner toward Stuart Avenue. The lights were very bright. The shithead covered his eyes."

Cal ran down the dirt path.

"Everybody, please, join me in looking for the gun."

They all tentatively walked down the path that was now muddy from yesterday's torrent. After a while, Little Brother held up the gun.

"Found it! Found it!" he yelled.

"Bring it here!" Cal yelled.

Little Brother ran to Cal.

"Is this it?"

"Yup, that's it"

"Is it loaded?"

Cal pulled the trigger five times.

"Nope. I emptied the chamber before I threw it," Cal said.

"Let's get out of here. I don't like it," Frannie said.

They trotted towards the Jesus house. Little Brother suddenly got down on his knee and aimed the gun at the corner.

"Bang! Bang! Bang! You're dead!"

Cal and the others scooted past the white propane tanks and went through the kitchen door.

"Jesus. What was that about? I mean the gun?" Charles said.

Little Brother plopped it on the table.

"Here it is. Take a good look."

"What shall we do with it?" Charles asked.

"It's mine, finders keepers," Little Brother said.

Frannie put her hand gently on the gun. She shivered. "Joey will be home soon," she said.

Little Brother began to cry. "But I found it," he said.

"Little Brother, we always decide things by family counsel," Frannie said.

Little brother pouted.

Joey came in through the kitchen door. It must have been raining because his jacket was wet. He hung it up carefully in the pantry, turned and closed the pantry door.

"What the hell is that," he said, pointing to the gun.

"Little Brother found it. Now he wants to keep it," Frannie said.

"It should be with Emma. That's where we keep our firearms, isn't it?" Little Brother said.

"Let's have a family vote. We always have a vote on serious topics," Frannie said.

"Do I get a vote?" Cal asked.

"No, you're not a family member," Little Brother said.

"What about me?" Charles asked.

"The same goes for you, Charles," Frannie said.

"I thought we had an agreement," Charles said.

Frannie blushed.

"We don't, Charles. Not anymore."

Charles stared at Cal.

"Oh, is that what is going on?"

Joey hit the table hard.

"Back to business," Joey said. "Cal and Charles do not have votes. I am chair, and the question is, should we keep the revolver?"

Frannie hesitantly nodded.

"Yes, I think so too, for all of our use," Joey said, glaring at Little Brother.

Little Brother banged the table with his forehead.

"I found it. I should keep it. That's the rule around here."

"That has never been the rule around here," Frannie said.

Little Brother got up and slammed the table. He marched off upstairs to the bedroom he shared with Joey.

"I'll take this in to Wausau Gun and Tackle, see what they say about it."

"Well, I guess that's the conclusion," Charles said. He stood and shook hands with Joey. "Nice going, boss."

Charles went to the kitchen door.

"Shouldn't we at least have talked about this, Frannie?"

"Charles, I'm very sorry."

"Maybe tomorrow?" Charles said.

"Maybe, maybe tomorrow."

Charles kissed Frannie on the forehead. Frannie blushed. Charles went out the door.

Chapter 9

The next day, Cal walked with Joey to the Piggly Wiggly. They scrutinized the awning, which kept the light rain off them.

As manager, Joey opened the door and looked around carefully. He went to the two cash registers and checked the figures twice. He was satisfied, so he signed and dated them both. Then he opened the door to the stock room, took a mop and bucket, and cleaned the stock room floor, especially the ladies' room.

"I have to do all of that?" Cal asked.

"Oh, and more, much more," Joey said.

It was 7:30 AM, and the door into the stockroom opened from the outside. Wilkins, an Ojibwe with a very dark complexion and a beige raincoat, came in carrying a heavy canvas bag full of meats and fish — venison, beaver, muskrat, and raccoon. He smiled uncertainly at Cal, who waved back in a friendly manner. Wilkins sat down at Joey's desk in a white metal folding chair.

"Put it all on my desk," Joey said.

Cal was curious as to what the meats were.

Edna, the principal cashier, came in.

"Good morning, boss" she said, grinning.

She hung up her black raincoat and put her umbrella on the umbrella stand by the door. She had brown hair cut short.

She put a white metal weighing scale on Joey's desk. She weighed the meats and wrote down the weights on a paper pad. She showed the paper pad to Joey, who didn't bother looking, and to Wilkins, who studied the numbers and then nodded.

"Show the numbers to Cal," Joey said.

Edna turned and showed the numbers to Cal.

"Is that a good haul?" Cal asked.

Wilkins nodded.

"Very good."

Edna paid Wilkins, who politely thumbed through the dollar bills. Wilkins and Edna carried the meats in pink butcher paper and put them in a special glassed section at the end of an aisle where a sign read Game Fish & Meats. Then Wilkins pointed to Cal and motioned him to bring the other meats, which Cal did.

Joey turned to Cal.

"I have an errand to do. Won't be but a twenty-minute drive both ways."

"Joey, you're not going to leave me here on my own, are you?" Cal said.

"It's the first part of being a manager, and Edna knows a lot. You can rely on her."

Joey got into his blue and yellow Datsun pickup truck and sped away down Third Avenue. He parked, got out, and knocked on a door carrying red flowers. The door opened. A slightly chubby blonde woman stared at him.

"Joey Sienkiewicz."

"May I please come in for a while?"

"You've always been able to come in, Joey."

"Yes, I know that now."

A three-year-old toddler ran out of a bedroom. His pajamas covered his feet.

"Jeremy! Daddy is here."

"Daddy!"

He held out his arms. Joey picked him up.

Joey had tears in his eyes. He sat in a red easy chair. He lifted little Jeremy onto his lap. Jeremy giggled when Joey tickled Jeremy's tummy. Roberta sat opposite him. There was a very long silence.

"How have you managed, Roberta?"

"I am an unwed mother so I get a stipend."

"I am so very sorry for the way it turned out."

"I know you feel bad, Joey."

There was another long pause during which Roberta studied Joey some more.

"Do you want to get married, Joey?"

“Is that possible?”

“Jeremy is a Lutheran. He will never be Catholic.”

Joey did not know what to say, until Jeremy hugged him around the neck. “Yes, that’s alright, Roberta. Isn’t it, Jeremy?”

Jeremy nodded.

“Emmanuel Lutheran. We sang songs today, didn’t we?”

“Beautiful songs!”

Joey patted Jeremy on the back. Joey’s eyes were getting moist.

“Are you sure about this, Joey? It’s been a long time you know,” she said. Her voice trembled.

“I’ve never been so sure.”

Joey sat at the kitchen table.

“I’ve been promoted to manager of the Piggly Wiggly!”

“What did you have to do to get that?”

“Mr. Zimbauer died.”

“Where there’s death, there’s hope,” Roberta said. “You must be hungry, Joey,” she added.

She got up to go to the kitchen.

“Don’t bother, Roberta.”

Roberta made two fried eggs, buttered some toast and poured some strong coffee into a mug that read in blue letters All Hallows Lutheran Church. She brought it round to Joey and fed him. Jeremy twitched but did not wake up. Roberta dabbed at Joey’s face with a napkin and took the plate back into the kitchen sink.

She sat back in her red easy chair. The light was diffused coming through the north window. There was a pretty carpet, gray with moose heads. There was a kitchen table under a window by the south side. The bedrooms were deep in the apartment. Jeremy slept in a crib next to Roberta’s bed. There was a New Testament next to an Old Testament on the shelf by Roberta’s bed.

“How can I earn your trust after all this time?”

“Frankly Joey, I don’t think you can.”

“Can I at least come by to see Jeremy?”

“Of course, he’s your child.”

* * *

At the Piggly Wiggly, Marcie, the second cashier, came in. She had auburn hair, cut short like Edna's. She also wore garnet earrings. She grinned and waved to Cal and Wilkins. She sat beside Edna.

"Where did the boss go?" Marcie asked.

"He had an errand, with Roberta I presume," Edna said.

"Who's in charge?" Marcie said.

"I guess we all are," Edna said.

The door opened. Mrs. Jacobson, folding her wet umbrella and putting it in the umbrella stand by the door, came in smiling. She looked around for Joey but did not find him.

"He's on an errand to his beloved. He'll be back in a second or two," Edna said. Mrs. Jacobson grinned and walked into the aisles.

Other customers began coming into the store. After a while, Marcie stood up and yelled for Edna. Edna turned. Marcie pointed to a young man with long brown-blond hair and motorcycle boots.

"Cal!" Marcie yelled.

Cal turned.

"He ain't supposed to be in here," she said.

Cal walked up, stood chest to chest with the man and gave him a push backward.

"You're Jack Monday, aren't you?"

The guy pushed back.

"Don't do that, Cal. We used to be buddies."

"Yeah, and then you tried to drown me in the municipal pool."

"It was only three feet deep."

Cal tried to escort Jack out the door. Jack shook himself free and demanded barracuda.

"We don't sell barracuda," Edna said.

"Why not?"

"Nobody supplies it to us."

"Well, that's a shame in bed, isn't it? I want some barracuda. That's what I came for."

"We have beautiful largemouth bass on special."

Marcie and Edna took turns pointing out the fish. Something

about the procedure caught Wilkins's attention, especially when the fellow pushed Cal.

"Where's the damn barracuda?" he shouted.

Customers turned to see what was going on.

"Keep it quiet, Jack, this is a family store, and I don't think you're really welcome," Cal said.

Jack went out of control and grabbed as much of the fish as he could in his arms.

Once again, Cal tried to push Jack toward the door, but Jack resisted.

"Let me go!" he shouted. "I'm Jack Monday!"

All the customers were glued to the drama along the fish aisle, especially since Jack Monday was now throwing the fish specials onto the floor and at Cal.

Cal slipped on the fish-squirmy floor. Jack Monday grinned in glee and began stomping on Cal's stomach. Cal groaned with every thump of Jack's motorcycle boot, trying desperately to twist and turn out of Jack's way, but Jack kept stomping and grinning.

"Pink panties!" Jack yelled, "Pink panties! Isn't that what you said I was wearing?"

He stomped again.

Wilkins stood from Joey's desk. He walked slowly down the adjacent aisle and around. He grabbed Jack Monday by surprise and with his right arm around Jack's neck, his left fist bashed into Jack. It broke Jack's nose, which spurted blood onto the aisle. A woman screamed.

"You broke it!" Jack Monday yelled.

Jack fell to his knees and groped.

At that moment, Joey's blue and yellow Datsun pulled up to a stop outside the door. Joey jumped out.

"What the hell is going on?" he yelled.

Cal, holding his stomach, leaned forward and vomited on Jack's face.

"The police are here," Edna said.

Joey pointed to Jack, who was struggling to get level with the fish.

"Officer McKinney. I know you," Jack said, bewildered.

"Unfortunately, Jack, I know you, and I can tell you where you're going," the officer said. He pulled his handcuffs off his black belt, and while Jack was still woozy he locked Jack's wrists together behind Jack's back.

Jack kicked at the cop's legs. "I don't wanna go."

"Well, you ain't staying here Jack," the officer said.

Officer McKinney took Jack to the patrol car and unlocked the rear door. Jack turned to run, but a second cop caught him and threw him back. He and Officer McKinney dumped Jack in the rear seat. Jack kicked wildly.

"I'm going to bleed all over your car!" Jack yelled.

The cops slammed the door shut and got into the front seats. Officer McKinney turned the ignition on. The patrol car, red light turning, went down Third Avenue to Thomas Street and turned left.

Joey walked carefully over the fish slime and addressed customers who had gathered to watch.

"Don't worry, folks, it's okay now. I am Joey Sienkiewicz. I'm the new manager. This guy we know too well. He's a hood and a thug. He should never have been let into the store. The cops are hauling him to the police station right now ... The fish are on sale today. Marcie, and Edna, our cashiers, are washing them now. Wilkins, take Cal home."

"Where do you live?" Wilkins said.

"Down Third, to Stuart, turn right, there's a long lawn and then you can see my kitchen on your right."

"Sorry Joey," Cal said.

Wilkins grabbed Cal from under both arms.

"Come on, cowboy, back to the ranch."

Joey called Frannie.

"Frannie, we've had some trouble here at the store. Jack Monday came in. He wasn't supposed to. Cal and Jack had an old feud and Jack started beating up on Cal who couldn't defend himself. I've asked Wilkins to guide him home."

Chapter 10

Cal stumbled across Third Avenue, holding his stomach. Wilkins held out his right arm to stop the traffic on Third Avenue. With his left arm, he held Cal around the waist.

Once they stepped on the sidewalk, Cal spit up a little bit. He barely missed Wilkins.

"I can't make it, Wilkins," Cal groaned. "I'm all busted up."

Wilkins pulled Cal over the long, green, grassy way toward Frannie, who was brightly lighted in the glass paneled Sienkiewicz kitchen door. She was horrified. She opened the paneled door. Wilkins carefully hauled Cal into the kitchen.

"Is there a bed we can put him in?" Wilkins said.

"Follow me."

She led Wilkins, who was still supporting Cal, down the short corridor past the home altar, turning right into the living room and to the bed they had made for Cal.

"Lock all the doors," Cal said.

"You're safe here, Cal." Frannie said.

"I said, LOCK ALL THE DOORS!"

Wilkins locked the Third Avenue door. Frannie locked the kitchen and pantry door.

"*I am Wilkins. I punched out Jack Monday in Piggly Wiggly and brought you here to the Jesus house,*" Wilkins whispered quietly into Cal's ear.

Cal relaxed. He reached out.

"*Wilkins . . .*" Cal whispered.

Cal held onto Wilkins's arm with both hands.

"Take care of me, Wilkins."

"I'm going to practice some Ojibwe spiritual medicine on you. Is that okay?"

"Oh, please, Wilkins," Cal said.

Wilkins sat down cross-legged on the black and white linoleum floor and began chanting quietly in Ojibwe.

Joey tapped at the kitchen door. Frannie jogged out to the kitchen. She saw it was Joey and let him in.

"Where were you, Joey? What kind of errand were you on?"

"Never mind, where's Cal?"

"Follow me."

She led Joey into the living room. He put a hand on Wilkins's shoulder.

"What's going on?" he asked.

Frannie turned. "Shhh, it's an Ojibwe medicine chant to improve Cal's spirit."

"*Kurwa*," Joey said.

He telephoned Dr. Belfour, the family doctor.

"Could I speak to Dr. Belfour, please? It's Joseph Sienkiewicz."

Joey asked Dr. Belfour to come right over to the Sienkiewicz home and to bring some painkillers, because the fellow they had redeemed from homelessness got beat up.

"Joey, who's taking care of the Piggly Wiggly?"

"Edna. Now calm down."

The kitchen door rattled.

"My, that was quick," Frannie said.

Joey unlocked the kitchen door. It was Little Brother who barged in.

"Why are you locking the doors?" he said. "And what is that chanting? Is that a medicine man?"

"Go to the living room," Joey said.

Little Brother went to the living room. When he saw Cal's gray face, he crossed himself. Little Brother touched Cal's cheek. It was freezing again.

After a while there was another tap on the kitchen door. Little Brother ran to the door. It was Dr. Belfour. Dr. Belfour had black hair and black eyebrows over dark, black eyes. He wore a black overcoat touched lightly at the shoulders with white snow. He carried a black medical bag.

He draped his overcoat onto Little Brother's shoulders.

"Where's the patient?" he asked.

Little Brother pointed down the corridor to the living room.

"Oh dear," Dr. Belfour said when he saw the color of Cal's face.

"He's cold too," Little Brother said.

Dr. Belfour put his hands gingerly on Cal's stomach. Cal groaned. Dr. Belfour prodded Cal gently. Cal groaned some more and rolled away because of the pain.

"He needs a hospital. Is it alright if I call for an ambulance?" Dr. Belfour said to Joey.

"Yes, please. The sooner, the better," Joey said, "here is the phone."

"No … not a hospital," Cal groaned.

"We can take care of him here, Joey," Frannie said.

"No we can't," Joey said. "Anyway, the ambulance is on its way."

Frannie sat on the edge of the bed, embracing Cal, who murmured affectionately.

"Don't worry, I won't let them take you away," Frannie said.

"The hell you won't," Joey said.

Joey felt Cal's ankles. They were cold. He rubbed Cal's feet. "I don't want him to die in my house," Joey said.

"He's not dying." Frannie said.

Cal groaned and rolled onto his side.

"Oh god. Oh god, please don't hurt me like this."

There was a knock at the door. Little Brother went to open it. It was the ambulance crew. One of them held a stretcher.

"Is this the Sienkiewicz residence?"

"It's a mistake that you're here. He doesn't need a hospital," Frannie yelled.

The stretcher holder looked confused.

"Do you want the stretcher or not?"

"Yes, we do, quickly. He's in very bad shape," Joey called from the bedside.

Joey came to the kitchen door.

"I am Joseph R. Sienkiewicz, the manager of the Wausau Third

Avenue Piggly Wiggly. He was hurt by a thug in the Piggly Wiggly premises. Come follow me and get him into a hospital quickly."

"What's that chanting we hear?" one of the crew asked as they came in.

"It's Cal's Ojibwe friend who is trying to increase Cal's spiritual strength. He no longer has the power of discrimination," Joey said.

* * *

Frannie blocked the way into the corridor. Joey put his arms around her waist and lifted her away from the corridor.

"He's in the living room at the end of this corridor," Joey said.

The ambulance crew apologetically walked past Frannie and through the kitchen. One crew member must have been Catholic because he pointed at the home altar and crossed himself.

"Bless you for coming so quickly. I am Dr. Belfour, the family doctor. I was the one who called you. I was authorized to do so by Joey. I am thrilled you're here and can take Cal to Memorial Hospital to be diagnosed and treated. I think something is ruptured in his stomach. It's very tender, so be good to him. He's in a lot of pain."

The crew placed the stretcher by Cal's side and raised Cal while sliding the stretcher under his side with utmost care. They put a strong painkiller into Cal's mouth. He tried to spit it out but they held his mouth open and it went down.

"They've poisoned me, Frannie, they've poisoned me. They're going to kill me in the hospital."

"No, you can't do that," Frannie said, grabbing hold of the stretcher bearer and yanking him away.

Joey embraced Frannie and pulled her away.

"Easy, duckling, it's all for the better this way. We can't cure the guy or even diagnose him."

"Have you ever been in a hospital? It's terrifying," Little Brother said.

"It is for the better, Frannie. I don't have the equipment or training to find out what's really wrong, but the hospital does,"

Dr. Belfour said. "So, please. I have known your mother and father for a long, long time, and they were very decent about these things. We can't let the patient dictate."

Frannie burst into tears. While holding her tighter, Joey gestured for the crew to quickly take Cal out into the ambulance, which they did. Little Brother followed closely, watching carefully.

"Don't hurt him," Little Brother said, "he's my brother, and I love him."

Little Brother ran after them down the corridor, out the kitchen door, and down the sidewalk past the white propane tanks. The ambulance crew had already opened the ambulance's rear door. They carefully hoisted Cal upward on a metal ramp, hauling him inside.

An ambulance driver bolted Cal's stretcher to the floor and to the side wall, then he tugged on the red webs around Cal's chest. They were secure. Cal began to mumble, losing his coherence.

"What did you give me? What kind of poison was it?"

The driver slammed the rear door shut. The other fellow raised the metal ramp and then ran around to his side of the ambulance next to the driver.

"Off we go," he said.

Little Brother began crying. The ambulance engine started, and with a bump that made Cal groan, turned on the siren and, with the red light turning and shining on the roof, went quickly over the Stone Street Bridge and turned right toward Memorial Hospital. The river was black and choppy. Snow was falling heavily.

Cars pulled over. The ambulance pulled into the emergency entrance. A driver pressed a red button at the side of the emergency door. A nurse opened the door.

"What have we here?" she said.

"The family doctor thinks something is ruptured in his stomach."

"Take him to x-ray, please, and bring in Dr. Kavanagh."

The x-ray room was predictably dark. A technician adjusted

an 8x10 blank film in a black wood frame shielded by glass over Cal's stomach. He put another over Cal's lower abdomen. Cal was wriggling. He had been strapped in with blue rubber chords, they were elastic but they did not move beyond a certain point. It made Cal claustrophobic. He tried to get out.

"No, no," the technician said. "Stay where you are and don't move or we just do this over and over again."

The technician put an x-ray film on Cal's head and neck. He carried the films to a side door. He knocked and opened the door. A white gloved hand reached out from the dark room and took the exposed film. The door closed.

The technician came back. He put a hand on Cal's shoulder.

"You'll be alright my friend, but you're blinking out now and then. Dr. Kavanagh won't like that so be still. We'll just wait a few minutes while these develop."

"I hurt. I hurt. I hurt," Cal said. "Their painkiller wasn't very good, I know about these things."

Dr. Kavanagh came in. He was a short, round doctor with rimless glasses. He spoke and moved quickly. He went to the white door.

"Are we developed?" he asked.

"Just about," said a voice from inside the developing room.

After a while, the door opened. The gloved hand handed Dr. Kavanagh four exposed plates. Dr. Kavanagh took them to the brightly lighted technician's booth and examined the plates, holding them up to the light. He held a loupe to his eye and over the exposed film plate.

"I think they've got the fifth exposure ready for us," the technician said. "I'll get it, Dr. Kavanagh."

He knocked on the door.

"Technician, can I have the fifth exposure, please?"

The technician took the frame with the exposed and fixed plate and brought it to Dr. Kavanagh, who looked at it.

"This is no good, he must have moved."

"Shall we do this again, Dr. Kavanagh?"

"Please give me an unexposed plate."

Dr. Kavanagh took it to the plate and knocked.

"Dr. Kavanagh here. I want to give you the fifth plate to be exposed and fixed."

The door opened. A white gloved hand reached and took a film, took it into the dark room, and closed the door.

Dr. Kavanagh went back into the bright technician's booth. Once again he studied the exposed film with the help of his loupe.

The technician went back to the white development room door. When it opened the white gloved hand gave him the last exposed plate which the technician hustled to Dr. Kavanagh.

"Thank God there's no actual rupture ... just some bad bruises. Drop of blood on the brain. How did that happen? I want to keep him here for four days for observation."

A porter arrived.

"Ward Seventeen," Dr. Kavanagh said as he led while the porter wheeled Cal into Ward Seventeen.

The porter unlocked the door of Ward Seventeen and moved Cal's bed into an empty space by the window. There were men in the other eight beds. Some were groping. A nurse came into the ward. She had a nurse's hat and a matching dress, all in blue and white. Three men whistled. She walked briskly to Cal and held out a paper cup. Cal stared bleakly at her.

"What the hell is this?" he demanded.

"It will relax you."

"Bullshit."

Dr. Kavanagh raised a finger.

"Easy does it, my friend," Dr. Kavanagh said. "It's Lorazepam. It's very light."

"I've taken Lorazepam, it's not good for anything," Cal said.

Cal was wary, but the nurse put the medicine cup into his mouth and tilted it.

"Down it goes," she said.

Dr. Kavanagh sat on a chair and put his hand against Cal's cheek.

"You're warm."

"I wanna go home," Cal said.

"You will, but not right now," Dr. Kavanagh said. He looked at his clipboard. "Well, praise the Lord, nothing is ruptured, but I imagine you're in pain."

"Damn right!"

"You have some bruises on your lower stomach, but your abdomen is okay. There is a drop of blood on your brain. I wouldn't worry about that."

"Of course not. It's not your brain."

"Take it easy Cal, the tranquilizer will start to work very soon. If it doesn't, I'll give you a painkiller. You'll sleep till dawn at least."

"Tranquilizer. Doctor, I want tranquilizer," one of the drug addicts called from across the room.

"I'm going to keep you here for observation for three or four days. We have to be careful you know. Would you like some soft food?"

"No."

Cal was beginning to relax. Dr. Kavanagh untied the blue rubber restraints.

"Don't tie me up again. You'll be really sorry," Cal said.

The sun was starting to go down. There were long shadows from the beds of Ward Seventeen. Dr. Kavanagh finished reading from his clipboard.

"Cal, I understand that you have taken mescaline, marijuana, LSD."

"Acid! Nurse, bring me some acid! I'll be nice to you!" One of the drug addicts yelled.

Dr. Kavanagh turned. "Don't yell at the nurse, Henry."

The nurse grinned and walked out the door. Cal closed his eyes and snored just a little. He slept. When he opened his eyes Dr. Kavanagh had gone.

Cal got up. He was wobbly and sat down quickly. He got up again, very slowly. He got into slippers that were by his bedside. He felt his way to the door. It was not locked. He peered both ways up and down the corridor. He walked out, sliding his slippers against the wall. He went down toward reception. He tried unlocking the main door, but it wouldn't budge. He turned.

"Receptionist, somebody has locked the door. Dr. Kavanagh said I need some fresh air."

The receptionist tried to call Dr. Kavanagh but could not get through.

"He's in surgery right now."

"Well, can I at least have some fresh air?"

"Okay, but five minutes, no more, or we will come out with a butterfly net."

The receptionist unlocked the door. Cal slipped out and went quickly down to the main sidewalk on Grand Avenue. It was very dark and very cold. He didn't know which way to turn. He kept turning his head left and right. A stranger in a gray raincoat stopped.

"Are you lost?" the stranger said.

"Which way to the Stone Street Bridge?"

The fellow pointed to Cal's left.

"Should you be out? You're still wearing hospital pajamas and slippers."

"Oh yes, the doctor said I could go home."

"I don't believe you."

"His name is Dr. Kavanagh. He's in surgery now. Please take me to the Stone Street Bridge."

The stranger hooked elbows with Cal. Together, they walked very slowly. The weather stick showed green, meaning colder tomorrow. The top red light was flashing, meaning snow or rain tomorrow. They passed Gowns by Carole, La Cantina, and then went past the Hotel Wausau on the street corner. Cal nearly fell. The stranger held him up.

"Easy, my son."

The stranger walked him to the Men's Shelter

"This is as far as I go," the stranger said. "But they'll take good care of you here. They'll feed you and keep you warm."

The stranger knocked and opened the door. There was a slight hum of activity in the Men's Shelter. American flags hung from the walls in the lobby and near the dining room. A warm draft of air moved into Cal's face. The stranger led Cal to a vinyl cushion seat and sat him down.

Cal slowly warmed up. He stopped shivering. Mr. Dula, a short man with hair brushed upwards and a big smile on his round face, came in quickly. The stranger left.

"Bless you, sir," Cal said.

The stranger raised his left hand in farewell, turned right, and was gone.

Chapter 11

"Hi sir, my name is Mr. Dula. Are you hungry?"

"No."

A tall young man with soft green eyes and light brown hair combed neatly sat on a vinyl chair next to Cal. He wore fine slippers and his trousers were neatly pressed, and so was his maroon shirt. He smiled and put a hand on Cal's left hand.

"Hi, I'm Ralph. I'm the unofficial assistant here. I sleep here and eat here, but I work at Brooks Men's Clothiers on Third Avenue during the day. Tomorrow I can bring you some proper clothing."

"Thank you, Ralph," Cal said.

"What's your name?"

"I'm C . . . Cal."

"His name is Cal," Ralph said to Mr. Dula.

"I know, I heard. Let's take him for a coffee and a shower."

In the dining room, two veterans sat close together drinking coffee. They both wore red poppies in their lapels. One of them watched Cal and tapped his poppy.

"Take it easy Fitz, he's just arrived," Ralph said.

"Well, tomorrow is Veterans Day, and I expect him to be outfitted appropriately."

Ralph and Mr. Dula both held Cal under the elbows.

"Ignore him," Mr. Dula said.

They carefully lifted Cal to his feet by the armpits. He leaned against Ralph. Ralph stroked Cal's back.

"Oh, that feels nice," Cal said.

"Are you okay? You seem a bit wobbly," Mr. Dula said.

Cal nodded.

"I'm okay," he said. He held out his right wrist. "Can you please cut off this hospital band?"

Ralph reached into a drawer at the reception desk and pulled out some scissors. He cut off the plastic identification bracelet around Cal's wrist.

"Thanks," Cal said.

"Would you like some coffee?" Mr. Dula asked.

"Love some," Cal said.

Ralph put the scissors away, and poured a Dixie cup of hot black coffee.

"Milk or cream or sugar?"

"No, just black."

"The way the Lord intended," Ralph said.

Mr. Dula came up behind Cal and steadied him with both hands on Cal's hips.

"Go ahead, take a sip but be careful. It might be hot, hot, hot."

Ralph gingerly put the cup in Cal's right hand. He helped Cal put it to his mouth. Cal sipped but missed.

"Christ, that was hot," Cal said.

"The coffee is brewing all the time," Mr. Dula said. "You can always get more from the dining room."

The three of them walked down the corridor past rooms where homeless men sat, watched television, or listened to a radio in room thirteen, which was once part of a women's prison but now had no lock.

"Ralph, can you start the shower please? Make it good and hot," Mr. Dula said.

Ralph went in and turned on the shower.

"I'm going to wash you, Cal. Undress please," Mr. Dula said.

Cal went to the corner of the room and turned his back on Mr. Dula and Ralph. He undressed, shielding his private parts. He tossed the hospital pajamas on the floor. Ralph scooped them up.

Mr. Dula put a hand under the shower.

"Too hot!" he said and quickly withdrew his hand. "What are you trying to do, Ralph? Roast the poor guy?"

Mr. Dula turned the shower control and put his hand back under it.

"Oh, that's better. Cal, my lovely. Come get showered properly."

Cal walked gingerly from the corner, still shielding himself. Mr. Dula put a white wicker chair under the shower.

"Have a seat, sir."

Cal sat under the hot shower. Mr. Dula handed him a soap which lathered easily and then a shampoo which also lathered easily.

Cal bent his head forward. His hair got thoroughly rinsed and hot. Mr. Dula worked in some cold shampoo and rinsed Cal's hair vigorously with the handheld showerhead.

"No lice in this camp," Mr. Dula said.

Mr. Dula gave the bottle to Cal.

"Listen to me Cal, this is soap. I want you to put it all over, you understand. All over."

"Yes sir."

"Especially your middle part and derriere. Understand?"

"Yes sir. Please don't look at me."

Mr. Dula turned away. "I've seen everything," he said.

Cal stood up and lathered himself all over. He held on to the white wicker chair for balance. He took the handheld shower head and rinsed his hair, chest, legs, especially the private parts.

"Oh, ha ha ho ho, you should try this Mr. Dula. It's great."

Cal lathered himself absolutely everywhere and rinsed absolutely everywhere.

"Look, I'm getting a hard-on."

"Well don't show it to me," Mr. Dula said.

Mr. Dula turned off the water. He handed Cal a large bath towel.

"Dry yourself thoroughly Cal, then step into these men's shelter thongs so you don't get water everywhere."

Cal did so. He was suddenly cold. He wrapped the towel around his shoulders.

"Don't we have shelter trousers and a shirt for our new friend?" Mr. Dula said

Ralph went into the corridor, opened a cabinet door, and piled his arms with trousers, a pajama shirt, and pair of shelter slippers. He brought them into the room.

Ralph slipped shelter briefs onto Cal.

"Just when we were starting to enjoy the view," Mr. Dula said.

Mr. Dula held Cal by the arm and shoulder while Ralph put on a cleanly ironed green shirt.

"Cal my boy, can you stand on one leg while we put the trousers on."

"Yeah, shoot."

Cal held onto Mr. Dula's arm and shoulder and raised his other leg, which Ralph deftly slid the trousers on. They were dark red. Ralph spread a sheet over the mat and plopped a clean striped pillow at the head end. Ralph came around behind Cal.

"Sit very slowly," Mr. Dula said.

Cal began sitting but flailed his arms. He held onto Mr. Dula as he went slowly down onto the sheeted mat. Mr. Dula covered Cal with another clean sheet. They put two wool blankets on the top of Cal.

"It's so strange in here, I can't sleep."

Mr. Dula opened a cabinet above Cal's head. He took out a bottle and shook out one pill.

Cal turned his head away. "No, I'm not going to take any more pills. I already took a Lorazepam today."

Cal closed his eyes but they popped open. Mr. Dula was still sitting there. Ralph was quite relaxed on his own bed. To Ralph's right was a scrawny diminutive figure who was affectionately called The Psychotic because of the black rings around his eyes. Cal slept.

* * *

Cal had a dream. In the dream a terrifically ugly woman with black hair and a black moustache who seemed to hate men had removed Cal's blankets and was trying hard to get him to urinate into a plastic urine bottle, but nothing came. The woman began to grow transparent. Cal rolled to his right and grabbed hold of Ralph.

"Are you alright, Cal?"

"No, I've had a nightmare. Can you hold me?"

Ralph held Cal.

"What was your nightmare? It's okay, you can tell me."

"The world's ugliest woman had slipped a cold plastic urine bottle onto my weenie. I couldn't pee."

"How do you know it was a nightmare?"

"She became transparent."

"You'll get used to those. After a while you can tell what's a hallucination and what's real."

Chapter 12

The next day was November 11, Veterans Day. Flags flew all down Third Avenue. There were two round metal flag holders on each side of the Piggly Wiggly's main door. Joey tried to put an American flag in each holder, but the wind had risen, and the cloth wrapped around his face so he couldn't see.

There were flags hanging from the other stores, all the way to the Esso station and Big Boy at Thomas Street. The mayor, a woman who wore a red paper poppy on her lapel, stood on the stage on the east side, which was a grass slope. She spoke to a closely packed audience. Veterans, many with American flags and red poppies pinned to their lapels, stood on the grass and watched. Fitz and Rafe were there, their arms around each other's shoulders. Finally, a boy from the high school band played "Taps." It was so sad and so beautiful. Tears were in many veterans' eyes as they remembered their friends who never returned. Tears were in widows' eyes.

"Now I'm going to the war memorial in front of the City Hall," the mayor said. "You can all join me to pay homage to those from Wausau who did not return."

The mayor stepped down from the stage and walked to the polished red granite war memorial in front of the old city hall, where she stood erect and saluted. Many in the crowd took the opportunity to find the names of those they knew.

The crowd dispersed very slowly. Many were sad. Many cried. All were silent. In the end, the mayor hugged everyone, man or woman.

Fitz and Rafe ambled over to the Hotel Wausau, which had a bar and round tables for its restaurant service on the ground floor. There were already many vets in there. The fellow behind the counter asked them what they would like. They ordered eggs and hash browns. Fitz and Rafe ate like there was no tomorrow, then began to walk to the door.

"Wait, wait, fellas, your payment!" the guy behind the counter said.

Fitz turned around. He pointed to his purple heart and his medal of honor and said, "You know what these are, sir."

"No, I have no idea."

Fitz rolled up his right trouser leg and then took off his orthopedic shoe and right sock.

"This is a Medal of Honor, and this is a Purple Heart. You get it for being wounded." He tapped on his artificial plastic foot.

It got very quiet. Fitz put his sock and shoe back on. Two veterans stood, and each gave Rafe and Fitz a ten-dollar bill.

"Thank you, American!"

Fitz and Rafe walked out to applause from most of the tables. They went around the corner to the men's shelter.

Mr. Dula gently woke Cal, who did not know where he was or who he was.

"Your first night here, Cal. How did it go? Did you sleep alright?"

"I had a hallucination."

"Was it frightening?"

"It sure was, but she's gone now. She got transparent and she disappeared."

Fitz and Rafe came down the corridor. Fitz pointed at Cal who was not wearing the red paper poppy.

"You ain't a patriot," Fitz said.

"I have some extra poppies. Would you like one?" Rafe asked.

Cal rolled over, holding onto Ralph again.

"What is it?" Ralph asked, "The nightmare come back?"

Cal nodded.

"They're at the door."

"Shall I get up and walk through them?"

"Thanks, but I'd rather hold you for a while."

Cal lay down again and tried to sleep.

"Mr. Dula!" Fitz called out.

Mr. Dula came down the corridor.

"What is it you guys want?"

"This fellow has no poppy. He has no American flag. Can you tell us who exactly he fought for?"

Mr. Dula escorted Fitz and Rafe back to the lobby.

"He has had his troubles too. Everybody here has had his own troubles. We don't criticize, we just want to get better."

Chapter 13

On November 15, Frannie telephoned the major hospitals, the local prison, and local mental health facilities. None had heard of Cal Bedrick. Frannie asked Joey to ask Wilkins if he had seen or heard from Cal. No luck. Little Brother suggested the men's shelter at the end of Stone Street Bridge.

Frannie called the men's shelter. Mr. Dula answered.

"Hello Mr. Dula, it's Frannie Sienkiewicz. I'm looking for a Cal Bedrick. He's missing. Is with you?"

"Yes Frannie, he is."

"Can I visit?"

"Of course."

She hung up the phone, crossed the dark river, and knocked on the men's shelter door. Mr. Dula answered. They hugged briefly.

"Have a seat Frannie, I had Ralph bring him in."

Ralph was sitting two seats away. Cal was sitting between Ralph and an empty chair for Frannie.

Cal wore Ralph's green shirt, brown trousers, a clean pair of socks, and new used shoes that were highly polished.

Frannie put a hand on Cal's forearm. She sat down next to him.

"Are you comfortable here, Cal? Wouldn't you rather come to the Jesus house where I can look after you?"

Cal looked anxiously at Mr. Dula.

"It's up to you, Cal. There are lots of veterans who would love to have your bed here."

Cal turned to Frannie.

"Who are you? What is the Jesus house?"

Frannie looked at Mr. Dula.

"Do you think he got shock treatment somewhere?"

"Possibly. He was wearing a hospital bracelet when a stranger showed him in."

"What should I do, Mr. Dula?"

"Come back in a few days. He's eating well and resting a lot. There's a lounge where he can watch TV and meet the other men. It's very comforting here after a while."

Frannie came back to visit Cal at the men's shelter several times. He began taking short walks over the river with Frannie.

"Cal, Thanksgiving is only a few days away. Please come to the Jesus house. Joey will bring potatoes, asparagus, and all kinds of good things in your honor."

They walked back to the men's shelter. They hugged briefly.

"Thank you, Frannie," Cal murmured.

"I care about you, Cal. November 27. You'll be there, right?"

"Actually, I can't, there will be a do at the men's shelter. I don't want to leave everybody."

"I understand, Cal."

Chapter 14

The Sienkiewiczes sat down for an early Thanksgiving dinner.

October had been a warm month. The Canadians celebrated their Thanksgiving while it was still warm. Americans, on the other hand, waited for the last Thursday in November, when it was cold, dark, and had often snowed. Families got together and watched television or got drunk and argued politics. The Sienkiewiczes however had no TV. There was no family feud amongst them, but something had changed the family tone: Cal Bedrick.

They crossed themselves. Frannie looked sad.

"What's the matter, kid?" Joey asked.

"Shouldn't we have invited a soldier or homeless person? That's what we used to do when Dad was alive."

"Well, Frannie ..." Little Brother said, "let's go to the shelter and bring Cal some turkey."

"Frannie darling, I've donated seven fresh turkeys from the Piggly Wiggly to the men's shelter. Not to mention the gallons of apple sauce, cranberry sauce, and apple cider. Cal has more than he can stomach."

"But shouldn't *we* give something?" Frannie said.

"What about fudge?" Little Brother said.

"Oh yes, the Halloween fudge!" Frannie stood up, waving her arm in distress. "Where the hell is the fudge? Where's the fudge? What did I do with the fudge?"

"Behind you, in the cabinet," Little Brother said.

"Oh, right."

Frannie opened the cabinet and pulled out a beribboned box of Piggly Wiggly fudge.

"Come with me, Little Brother."

"Right."

They put on their winter coats. It was raining. They put up their hoods and went out the kitchen door.

"Hey, what about me?" Joey asked.

"We'll be right back, Joey."

"You better be. I don't want to eat this turkey on my own."

Joey closed the kitchen door after them.

Frannie held the gift box of fudge. They went onto the sidewalk. Far ahead across the river was the weather stick on the bank's roof. It was very accurate and predicted tomorrow's weather. The electric lights showed green, which meant colder tomorrow. The top light was red and flashing on and off, which meant precipitation tomorrow.

Duck Island was deeply frosted everywhere, especially the lodge.

Frannie knocked eagerly on the men's shelter door and opened it. They went in.

Cal was sitting at the rear middle of the table in the large dining hall, like Jesus at the last supper. There was a hobo on his left and the two vets on his right, who wolf whistled when they saw Frannie.

Frannie gave a Sienkiewicz grin and waved her left hand.

"Hi Cal," she said as she walked to the table.

Cal was still weak, but he managed a hearty "Hi Frannie."

One of the vets patted his thighs.

"My name is Fitzsimmons. People call me Fitz. Sit here darling. I've saved it for you."

"My name is Rafe," a tall skinny vet with two deep scars on his left cheek who sat next to Fitz said.

"I'm going to sit next to Cal," Frannie said.

"Is that the way it is?" Fitz said.

"I'm afraid so."

Frannie went around the hobo and sat on the chair between him and Cal. She gave Cal a box of fudge. Cal and Little Brother took a piece each.

"Can we have a piece?" Fitz said.

Rafe laughed. There was a pause.

"Just one," she said.

Fitz and Rafe each took one piece and put it in their mouths.

"Mmm… Better than homemade."

There were many tables in the dining hall, but only half were occupied. Many homeless were probably out, having been invited by local residents for Thanksgiving dinner, or at a church dinner. The chef was busy behind a cutout window at the rear of the dining hall. He had served soft cranberry in silver plated cups and then returned to the chef's station. Coffee was now being served by young female volunteers, many of whom got pinched as they went by.

Fitz turned to Cal. "I'll bet you've never served in the army," he said.

"Nope," Cal said.

"What were you doing," Fitz said, "while other guys of your age were dying for their country?"

Little Brother's eyes were darting back and forth between Fitz and Cal. Frannie was getting tense. Her green eyes narrowed.

"Let's see. I was taking drugs. I threw rocks at the passing National Guard but missed. I threw a larger stone at the California Highway Patrol and smashed through their window."

"What did you do after that?" Little Brother asked.

"Ran like hell," Cal said.

"I'll bet you did," Rafe said.

Frannie leaned forward and looked at Fitz. She tapped the table for emphasis.

"Cal suffered just like you, not with bullets but with worse things. Mental suffering is always worse. He's been homeless, on the road for eight months. He never had an army, a helicopter, or a medic to look after him. It's only by the grace of God that he made it here where he grew up."

"Hallelujah," Fitz said sarcastically.

"I want you to respect Cal Bedrick," she continued, tapping her forefinger on the table with each syllable and staring into Fitz's eyes with her own narrow green cat's eyes.

"I will never accept people who didn't fight for their country," Fitz said

Mr. Dula chanced to be by the table. He looked at Fitz and Rafe and said sternly: "The war is over. We lost. Let it go."

"We didn't lose. We left. And the Communists overran the south," Cal said.

"Thanks, college boy," Fitz said.

"There are no conflicts in this men's shelter. We all get along. And if you can't, I will expel you," Mr. Dula said.

"And then you'll be really homeless," Little Brother said.

Fitz sank in his chair. "Okay, I get it Mr. Dula." Then he sat up, bright-eyed. "What's your name?" he said to Little Brother.

"Larry is my real name, but they call me Little Brother."

"Why do they call you Little Brother? Don't you see they're demeaning you so they can control you?" Fitz said.

"How old are you?" Rafe asked.

"Nineteen," Little Brother said as he flexed his biceps.

Fitz felt them.

"Oh my god, you're a manly beast. I'd go down first thing tomorrow morning and enlist in the army if I were you. Did you ever see my medals?" Fitz said.

"Oh no, show them to me."

Fitz opened his collar. There was a bronze Medal of Honor and a Purple Heart.

"Wow! How did you get those?"

"The hard way."

Fitz raised his right trouser leg and took off his sock to show his green plastic foot. "Tap it, go ahead."

"Wow, that's stronger than iron."

"You're right. It is."

"What happened, Mr. Fitz?" Cal asked.

"Well, we were bivouacked in our tents, trying to get some sleep any way we could. We were in dense foliage. We suddenly heard explosions. I woke up. I knew right away that the Viet Cong were on our side of the trip wires. I don't see how that could have happened, but I could sense it. I grabbed my pistol and ran out. Our sentries had had their throats cut. A slight fellow in black pajamas pulled the pin of his grenade, counted to three, and tossed it into a tent of sleeping GIs. I heard screams. Then I saw that two of them had been badly wounded on the legs and hips but crawled out anyway, looking for the enemy with automatic rifles.

"Our guys' automatic rifle bullets raked the lower tripwire and then traced an ugly path right through the bushes on my left. We heard more screams. We might have got them all. I never felt the grenade go off that took away my right foot. I heard but did not see a helicopter come down onto the dirt. I saw this guy Rafe, who was a medic, jump out of the helicopter as it was still descending,"

"Like a knight in shining armor," Little Brother said.

"Exactly. He ran over to me and tied a tight tourniquet on my right calf. He swabbed my right calf and then injected morphine into it. It began to hurt like hell. 'Can you feel your right foot?' he asked me. 'A little,' I told him. He gave me another shot of morphine and said, 'That's odd because you don't have a right foot.' "

"Did you feel the morphine?" Little Brother asked.

"Not at first. I was fading fast. I thought I was dying, but it was only the morphine. Rafe got some plasma into me, and I slightly revived, only to realize that I was being flown out to a hospital ship. I looked down at the water going by. We landed on the ship. Everything had been happening in slow motion. They took me to the Philippines. I stayed in that bed for about a week. That's what I was told. I practiced using a crutch. I was pretty clumsy. The next thing I knew, I was in San Diego in a VA hospital, and they were cleaning my wound as best they could. They tried on several sizes of foot replacements. This green one sort of fit, but it was painful to use, so they fixed up something made of foam between the rest of my leg and where my foot had been."

Little Brother was hypnotized. "Wow! I'd like a Purple Heart too, and a plastic foot."

"Well, come with us. We'll take you to the recruiting station in City Hall."

Little Brother looked at Frannie. She shook her head.

"Doesn't it hurt?" Cal asked.

"No, but it itches. I have to pour hot water between the skin that's left and the plastic. Sometimes it itches when I know there's no foot actually there."

"Very spooky," Rafe said.

"Listen, Little Brother," Cal said. "Lots of guys came home without legs without arms but also without their you know what. Thousands. I'll bet this war hero has lost something near and dear to him," Cal said. "They wake up in the hospital and ask the nurse, 'Where's my delta?' The nurse has to tell them, 'Your delta is gone.' "

Little Brother scrunched up his face and asked, "What's a delta?"

Fitz leaned to Little Brother. "It's your prick and balls."

Little Brother instantly covered his private parts.

"Ain't nobody ever going to take my prick and balls," he said.

"The enemy probably won't be aiming at your private parts but may hit them anyway. Bullets, mortars, grenades, shrapnel, and metal bits are flying all over the place, and you can never predict where they will hit." Cal leaned over to Little Brother. "Tens of thousands of young and otherwise healthy American men can't do it and probably pee through a tube into a bottle."

Fitz screwed up his eyes. "What the hell does that mean, college boy."

Fitz threw a cup of hot black coffee over Cal, but Cal ducked and covered Frannie. The coffee that spilled went on the hobo.

The hobo stood, red face pointing at Fitz, shaking with anger. "DON'T NOBODY NEVER THROW NO COFFEE AT BARNEY SCHULTZ."

Barney picked up his bowl of oatmeal and threw it at Fitz. It caught him by surprise and split his lower lip. A mixture of oatmeal and blood dribbled down onto his Purple Heart. Rafe tried to towel it away from the Purple Heart and the bronze Medal of Honor.

"You can't do that to me. I'm a war hero!" Fitz yelled.

"You're not a war hero!" Barney yelled back. "You're a war bum! Why else would you be here?"

Mr. Dula came running.

"Boys, boys, no fights. The war is over. This is a shelter for the mind and soul as well as the body. We must be gracious to one another, for we have all suffered. One more violent incident like this, Fitz, and I will expel you and Rafe from the shelter. I have authority to do so."

There was a pause. Fitz leaned again toward Little Brother. "Remember, girls want it too. They dig my plastic leg and Purple Heart." He turned to Frannie, who glared at him and then turned back to Little Brother. "Listen, Larry. The best whorehouses are in Saigon," Fitz said.

"What is a whorehouse?" Little Brother asked.

"You choose a girl, take her to a room, and pay her to do whatever you want with her. She's very compliant and will do whatever you ask. Vietnamese women are the most beautiful in the world."

"Is it expensive?" Little Brother asked.

"You could easily afford it on combat pay. There are also bars and restaurants. Not expensive at all by American standards."

"I'd like to go to a whorehouse," Little Brother said.

"No!" Frannie said.

"Come with us. We'll show you," Fitz said.

"Stay right where you are, Little Brother," Frannie said.

Fitz turned to Frannie. "I'm a real tiger and lion in bed. Girls have begged me for more."

"I said stay right where you are, Little Brother."

Fitz and Rafe stood. "Come with us. We'll show you what to do with women."

Little Brother started to rise, but Frannie put a hand on his shoulder and pushed him down.

"Goodbye, Rafe. Goodbye, Fitz," Frannie said.

The two vets walked to the door and went out but stood on the sidewalk.

"Come on, Little Brother, let's go home. Joey and the turkey are waiting for us," Frannie said as she stood. Cal put a wide left hand on her shoulder to say thank you. Frannie and Little Brother went out onto the bridge. It was already dark. The vets followed them.

"Can I enlist, Frannie?" Little Brother said.

"No, you'll get shot up. I'll lose you. The family will break apart."

She began walking faster, holding Little Brother's hand. "Hustle your buns, Little Brother. They're following us."

The bridge sparkled with snow powder, and so did the Junior Game Warden Lodge on Duck Island below. The island itself was slowly piling up with gentle snow. Some evaporated then blew away, some stuck. Tiny specs of snow melted on their faces. They were now running to the Sienkiewicz house. They both came in through the kitchen door. Joey looked up. The table was beautifully laid. Joey sat impatiently beneath the oil portrait of Jesus.

"Why the hell are you breathing so hard?" Joey asked.

"We were being followed over the bridge by two vets. They were coming after me," Frannie said, breathing hard.

"Yeah, they wanted her, sexually," Little Brother said.

"Oh, they did, did they?" Joey said. "Save my spot. I'll have a word with them." He stood and put on his high school basketball jacket. He went out of the kitchen door, closed it, and intercepted the two vets in the middle of the bridge.

The vets were on the left side of the sidewalk. Joey blocked them. The vets smiled and moved to the right. Joey blocked them again. Fitz got the idea, frowned, and said, "Yes?"

"I think you met my sister a little while ago? She has red curly hair and green eyes."

Fitz brightened. "Oh yeah, that's where we're going. Her green eyes were like a snake, but if you looked into them, you knew what she was thinking."

"What was she thinking?" Joey asked

I'm hot to trot.
And my twat is hot.

Joey's left fist smashed into Fitz's right jaw. Joey's right fist smashed into Fitz's left jaw. There was an audible crack. Fitz slid down against Rafe who could not quite hold him.

"He hurt me Rafe. He hurt me bad. Call a medic."

Joey took a couple of steps toward Rafe. Rafe held up both hands in self-defense and stepped backward.

"No, stop. I respected your sister. Ask her, just ask her. I am not a sex fiend."

Joey looked at him for a while. Rafe took another step back.

"Call a medic, for God's sake," Fitz said.

"I am a medic, but we're not in Vietnam now," Rafe said.

"Dial 911. Ask for an ambulance. You're in the middle of Stone Street Bridge," Joey said.

"Should I call the police?" Fitz said.

"I would so not do that if I were you," Joey said, "I know Mr. Dula well, we go to the same church. He's already told me about the trouble he's had with you two. The war is over, forget everything now."

"Y… y… yes sir," Rafe stuttered.

"Good, here comes the ambulance."

Joey turned and walked back to his home.

The ambulance stopped and picked up Fitz. You could see the crew inject Fitz with morphine. Rafe helped one of the crew men get Fitz to the metallic ramp. He called to the driver and the ramp went up. Fitz, the driver, and Rafe were all lifted simultaneously to the same height as the ambulance floor.

Joey went in the kitchen door and sat under the oil portrait of Jesus.

"Joey, your knuckles are bleeding." Frannie handed him two paper towels.

Joey laid the paper towels over the backs of both his hands and sure enough, red blood seeped up.

"You really told them, Joey," Little Brother laughed.

Joey caught his breath. He turned to Little Brother and put his blood-stained left hand on Little Brother's right shoulder.

"Little Brother, this is very serious. It's not a joke. That war has ruined our country. We lost the war, and America had never lost a war."

"Cal told Fitz we hadn't lost the war. We just left, and the Commies took over," Frannie said.

"I don't care what your boyfriend said. We lost the war, and worse, they had taken drugs and could not adjust to life back in the States. They're awful angry and cause physical trouble, not how it used to be. It has divided America worse than any civil war."

"Were you in the army, Joey?" Little Brother asked.

"Reserves."

"Let's say a prayer, then enjoy our meal," Frannie said. "May Jesus grant America peace. May Jesus look after our veterans and our soldiers. May Jesus bless the food we are about to eat. Amen."

They slowly lowered their hands from prayer. Joey was no longer breathing hard. Frannie smiled at him. Joey picked up the turkey carving knife, which was slightly curved and had a curved black plastic handle and a long curved blade.

"How was your Thanksgiving at the shelter?" Joey asked.

Frannie smiled brightly, "Oh, Cal was happy to see me, and I was happy to see him. He's physically improved."

"You have a crush on this guy, don't you?" Joey said.

"Yes," Frannie replied.

Joey picked up the turkey carving knife with both hands in samurai fashion over his head.

"*Banzai!*"

The knife went crashing through the turkey, dislodging a drumstick that Little Brother caught in the air. The blade cracked the souvenir serving plate that had read Warszawa. They all ate.

"This was a wonderful Thanksgiving, boys. If you don't mind, I'm going to shower and go to bed." Frannie said.

"Goodnight Frannie," Joey and Little Brother said in unison. They hooked their little fingers and gave a little tug.

Frannie laughed, stood, and walked to the stairs. She turned back and faced Joey.

"Joey, Cal Bedrick needs confidence. He needs some money. I feel this strongly. Give him another chance at the Piggly Wiggly."

"I refuse, Frannie. All he's ever done is read books."

"That's my point. You can teach him. Wouldn't that be the Christian way to do things, rather than him being helpless his whole life? Joey, please, for Dad. For Jesus. For me."

"You're nagging me, Frannie."

She gave him the Sienkiewicz smile. "It's our Christian duty, Joey."

Little Brother butted in. "Uh huh, she's right Joey."

Frannie went upstairs and into the bathroom, closed the door, and showered. She came out in a thick white terry cloth robe and came slowly downstairs and knelt at the home altar. She faced the Holy Mother.

"Please, Mother of God, look after Cal Bedrick." She stayed kneeling for a while, mumbling inaudible prayer. She slowly got up and turned to Joey.

"Joey, please. The Piggly Wiggly will need extra help leading to Christmas."

"Yeah, she's right, Joey," Little Brother said.

"Fine. Fine. Fine," Joey said.

"Thank you, Joey," Frannie said. She walked over to him and kissed him on the forehead.

"Jesus bless us all," Little Brother said.

Joey put his hand on her back and drew her closer. "Bless you, Frannie."

They looked at each other fondly for a long time.

"He can start December 2, but he has to shave, wash his hair, comb it, wear clean clothes, and give up his politics."

There was a long pause. Frannie turned and went to her room and closed the door gently.

There was a dresser on which there was a framed photograph of the Pope and a New Testament. To the left was a closet with folding white doors, and inside was a cardboard box of high school memorabilia.

Fannie went to the window. Duck Island was covered with a thick layer of fresh snow. She could see into the west channel. The trees were now bare. Once there had been a Baltimore oriole nest.

She went onto her bed, pulled the quilt over herself, and slept in her robe for extra comfort.

Chapter 15

Cal spent most of the days in the TV room. Ralph often sat with him. One day, Cal and Ralph took a walk down Third Street between Gowns by Carole, La Cantina, and on the other side, the stage. There were a few vets who were reading aloud the names of the dead men from Wausau.

"Is the war really and truly over?" Cal said.

"Unbelievable but yes," Ralph said. "Congress refused to budget for another year of war."

They walked to the Wausau Hotel and Bar on Bridge Street. The Wausau Hotel and Bar was a box-shaped building covered with blue and gray wall shingles. The top floor was black with tar paper and showed windows onto rooms where out-of-town visitors, mostly fishermen, stayed. The door was dark gray. The tavern was up a hill over the river. The sign outside was golden and advertised Blatz and above that said Wausau Hotel and Bar in small letters. They went in. There were no women except for the owner's wife behind the bar, which offered a range of beers: Paulaner, Münchner, Blatz, Miller High Life, Schlitz, and Hamm's.

A huge shellacked muskie hung in a varnished wood oval behind the owner's wife. A square white clock gave off a golden light that bathed the entire tavern. Fishing rods and fishing flies were on sale. There was a photograph of the owner's wife holding a huge walleye on a reed shore of Lake Wausau. There was another photograph of the owner, who seemed part native, in a red-and-black checked wool jacket and a red cap with earflaps. He had hammered a spout into a maple tree and was now collecting sap with a pail. It was in pretty woods with patches of snow and sunlight. Behind the photograph were five bottles of maple syrup, each labeled Wausau Hotel and Bar.

Ralph and Cal chose a pint of Blatz each and went to one of two old, slit maroon leather couches and sat down, putting their beer on thin cardboard coasters on the small table in front of them. They watched the bubbles rise in the glasses. One fellow came out of the men's room and began to play pinball. Cal and Ralph listened to conversations from the six or seven guys at the bar. According to the overheard conversation, the first black man in Wausau had been hired to be a chef at the Holiday Inn on the outskirts of town.

"Was he all alone?"

"Apparently."

"Well, you know, they have lots of cousins and uncles."

"Where's he from? Not down south I hope."

"I don't know."

"I hate the south, white or black."

"I hope we don't have to eat hominy and grits."

Men smiled.

"He's not gonna date my sister, I'll tell you that."

"I hate to tell you, Ed, but somebody has to," Ralph said.

Everybody laughed.

"*His sister is notoriously ugly,*" Ralph whispered to Cal.

Cal started to sing.

We're gonna hang Jeff Davis from a sour apple tree,
We're gonna hang Jeff Davis from a sour apple tree,
We're gonna hang Jeff Davis from a sour apple tree.

A few of the guy at the bar began to snicker. The woman behind the bar raised her right hand and looked at Ralph and Cal. The gesture meant *keep cool.*

Ralph went to the counter and paid for two ridged paper plates, each with a bratwurst and dollops of mustard, then brought them back to Cal with a paper napkin.

There was a disquieting rumor: The United States was transporting huge numbers of Hmong to Wausau. They were a tribe that had lived in the foothills between Vietnam and Laos. They had fought against the Communists and were in mortal danger now that the Communists had won.

"Where would they settle?"

"Probably the Hollow."

"It's too cold for them here," somebody in the crowd said. "There's no snow where they live."

"They'll take our jobs."

"You call what you do a job, Jim?"

It got quiet again.

They finished their Blatz. A man with scraggly hair and wide black eyes came in. It was the psychotic who slept on the other side of Ralph. He also ordered a Blatz and sat on a slit red couch.

"Do you need help getting home?" Cal asked.

"I am home. Leave me alone."

Ralph and Cal walked through the downtown past a tourist novelty store that sold sweatshirts bearing the white outline of Marathon County and Wausau. A huge arrow pointed to Wausau.

There was a nice-looking café called The Bluebird. They went under the marquee of the old grand cinema theater, which somehow had not been torn down, and then once again past La Cantina.

"Fancy a Mexican beer?"

"Well, are you buying?"

Ralph laughed. "Well, okay."

They went in and sat at a table. Ralph caught the eye of the Mexican woman behind the counter. There were tables and chairs on the far side of the room and space for dancing although nobody was dancing now. They had a Mexican beer each. Ralph looked at his watch.

"It's time I should go to Third Avenue on the other side of the river. This is Third Street where we are."

"I know, I know, I know. I remember now."

They got up. Ralph paid. They walked out, turned left, and turned left again onto Stone Street. The said farewell. Ralph went on to Third Avenue across the river and Cal went inside the men's shelter.

Chapter 16

The next morning Frannie went back to the men's shelter. Mr. Dula got Cal. Cal came out very sleepy on Mr. Dula's arm and shoulder.

"Look who's here," Mr. Dula said.

"Frannie!" Cal said.

"Did you sleep well?"

"Oh yeah, they gave me Lorazepam which is the same pill they gave me at Memorial."

Mr. Dula sat Cal down on one of the green easy chairs in the lobby. Frannie sat next to him smiling brightly.

"I'm so happy to see you, Cal. Are you happy to see me?"

"Sure."

"How's the food been?"

"Pretty good, pretty good."

"Joey said he's willing to hire you back at the Piggly Wiggly for two or three days per week as a stock boy. Please tell me you're willing to do that. This is a start. You understand me. It's a start."

Cal reluctantly nodded.

"Cal, take it, for heaven's sake, take it!" Mr. Dula said.

"I couldn't care for somebody who refuses to work," Frannie said. "Come to our house at 6 AM on Monday morning, then you and Joey can walk over to the Piggly Wiggly and open it up."

Ralph joined them. As usual, he was neatly dressed.

"Joey will pay you for the work you do. At first, it won't be a lot, but once you get better, it will build up. Isn't this why you came home?"

"Sure," he lied. She kissed her forefinger and touched his forehead. "From the bottom of my heart, Cal, I think this will be a good thing for you, and you will get paid. Money in your pocket you can do what you want with."

He put a hand on her hand. "Thank you for everything, Frannie."

"Mr. Dula. In the name of Jesus, I thank you. In a couple of days, Cal will be working part-time at the Piggly Wiggly as a stock boy for my brother Joey."

"Praise Jesus."

Mr. Dula crossed himself. So did Frannie.

Frannie spread her arms and they hugged, laughing gently and patting each other on the back.

Frannie leaned in to Cal.

"*Please come back to the Jesus house,*" she whispered.

"I will, I promise."

Frannie left the shelter, walked over the Stone Street Bridge, and took a little turn up First Avenue. She was very happy. A seagull walked ahead of her.

"Little birdie seagull, what are you doing here? You're two thousand miles from the nearest ocean."

She tiptoed to catch up to the bird, but the bird walked faster, then dived through the bare trees at the top of the bluff and waddled down to the old white wooden bridge and crossed onto Duck Island.

"Oh birdie, if I could catch you, I would hold you, love you, and protect you."

But the bird waddled away through the reeds and fallen leaves that were mostly covered in snow and then was gone. Frannie went home.

At 6 AM on the following Monday, Cal walked over the bridge to the Sienkiewicz house and had breakfast of scrambled eggs, toast with honey, and coffee.

Joey and Cal left for the Piggy Wiggly. When they got to the Piggly Wiggly, Joey opened the door.

"There's one thing only for you to remember Cal, and that is to do exactly what I say and to do it perfectly and quickly, and there will be no problems."

Joey took Cal into the stockroom and pointed out the cans of peaches, tomatoes, and soups of all kinds. He showed Cal where to stack them.

He took Cal out into the driveway out back where a farmer in a pickup truck had just driven in with asparagus. The truck was from Busom's, which was on Highway 51 going south.

"Follow me, Cal. I'll show you where they go."

Cal put the asparagus in the vegetable box.

"Now, Cal, what's missing?"

"I don't see anything missing."

"Carrots. There are no carrots here. Go back into the stock room and come back with an armful of bright, beautiful orange carrots. They go over there." Joey pointed to a green moss shelf.

Cal worked all day, asking customers what they were looking for. He was very pleased when he could help someone.

After a while, Joey beckoned to Cal.

"Look at this row of cans. What's wrong with them?"

"I don't know. Nothing."

"Look again."

"They look fine to me. All in good shape. I shelved them this morning."

"That's the problem. Now tell me which way the pictures on the can are facing."

"Every which way."

"That's the mistake."

He turned a few cans, so the picture of mushroom soup faced outwards.

"See, they should face outwards to show the customer what good things are in store."

"You mean in this store."

"Don't interrupt. I want you to go through this whole display of cans and make sure they are all legible to anyone."

Cal turned most of the cans around.

"Better."

Joey tapped his own forehead and mouthed the word *concentrate*. "This is how you learn to be a man, Cal. You concentrate on everything. You should have been in the army."

At the end of the day Joey sent Cal home to the Sienkiewicz house, where he had coffee and biscuits with Frannie.

"How did it go, Cal?"

"You have to ask the boss."

Frannie laughed. "Don't worry, I will."

Every day for the next week, until Pearl Harbor Day, December 7, Cal had breakfast with the Sienkiewiczes at 6 AM. There was a miniature American flag on the stand on the table. He was getting used to it. Snow began falling, small flakes at first and then bigger flakes, making indentations into the black water of the Wisconsin River.

The men's shelter observed Pearl Harbor Day. Donations from the city began arriving: a small Christmas tree with silver tinsel, shirts, trousers, socks, and shoes.

Frannie came by to see how Cal was doing. He put his arm around her waist. "Just fine Frannie, just fine," he said. "Give me a kiss."

She kissed him on the cheek.

"That's all?"

"It'll do for now. Cal, I'm here to invite you to Christmas dinner with us. After that, Joey, Little Brother, and I will go for Christmas mass. Maybe you can get something for Joey? He's been very nice to you. There's a stationery store called Emmons's downtown. Maybe get something there, a name plaque that says President or Manager. Wrap it or have them wrap it."

Cal began to work three hours each afternoon at the Piggly Wiggly — Monday, Wednesday, and Friday. He did not like the work, and he especially did not like taking orders from Joey.

When Cal received his first paycheck directly from Joey, he showed it to Ralph, who took him across the street to the bank to set up a savings account for most of it. Cal kept the rest.

Cal used some of the money at Emmons's, buying a large desk plaque that read "Manager" in white letters on a black background. It would stand up on Joey's desk.

"Could you please gift wrap this," Cal asked. "It's for my boss."

The clerk handed the desk plaque to one of the girls.

"Susanne, can you please gift wrap this, it's for this guy's boss."

"Please write the word "Boss" on the wrapping so he knows which one is his," Cal said. "It's a nice store you have here."

"Thanks, we do our best."

Chapter 17

It was December 24, Christmas eve. It rained lightly, but mostly it snowed.

The streetlights on both sides of the river were splendid. Downtown, lighted deer, Santa Clauses, candy canes, and snowmen hung from black electrical cords along the streets and dangled musically in the winter breeze. There were plastic snowflakes that twirled slowly but steadily. There were no religious decorations. At the Big Boy on the corner of Third Avenue and Thomas Street, the hired help wore elf costumes. The city hall was wildly decorated. The Esso station next to the Big Boy was decorated in red and green, and so was the mechanic's repair garage.

The skating rink in Marathon Park was busy with ice skaters. Christmas carols played loudly. There were cows and bulls in the agricultural building with tinkly bells on their horns. From Third Avenue to Stuart Avenue, every shop was brightly lit with yellow, red, and green miniature Christmas trees and window paintings of angels. The men's shelter had corrugated red and green bells on the door and inside the dining hall. On Duck Island, blue jays and red jays popped in and out of fir trees. Canada geese waddled over the lawn of the Jesus house.

Cal put on some socks and his shoes and went into the lounge of the men's shelter.

"Merry Christmas," Mr. Dula said.

"Merry Christmas," Cal replied.

Guys came into the lounge. They all got introduced. Ralph turned on the TV to a low volume. Mr. Dula left.

A city snowplow went slowly over the bridge.

The pregame show was underway. Ralph turned the volume up. On the television, somebody kicked a football. The Green Bay Packers and the Cleveland Browns ran toward each other. The guys in the lounge cheered, and so did the audience in Green Bay. Cal looked out the window, but it wasn't anywhere near dark yet. By half time, the Browns were ahead 9 to 6, and all the fellows except Cal went into the kitchen for lunch. Cal stayed where he was, looking mindlessly out of the window. The sky over the bank was blue and white.

The Green Bay Packer cheerleaders performed at half time, commentators with microphones spoke about the low score.

Somebody from the kitchen came in with a ham and cheese sandwich for Cal. Gradually the lounge filled up again. Half time was over. The football was kicked again, this time to the Packers. The crowd roared, and the guys in the lounge cheered. The cheeseheads, those Packers fans who wore mock cheese sections on their heads, yelled. Somehow the Browns scored a touchback and were given two more points, so it was 11 to 6.

There were tears and a few groans from the lounge. The Packers had the ball. The Browns were still ahead 11 to 6.. The Packers coach, Vince Lombardi, who wore his trademark black-rimmed glasses and long, gray raincoat, took the fingers of his right hand and banged them lightly into his left palm, signaling to the referee, *Time-out*. The Packers left the field and huddled around Lombardi, who knelt at the center of their circle. Everybody knew what was happening. It was going to be the last play of the game. Bart Starr, the quarterback, would throw a long Hail Mary pass into the end zone and hope for the best. The crowd stood on its feet, yelling for the Browns or the Packers. The referee circled his arm, which meant time would now resume. The Packers took the field for the last play of the game. The cheerleaders raised the cheers from the cheeseheads to a terrifying crescendo. Bart Starr took the snap from the center and backed up as if he would throw the end zone bomb, but he pivoted to the right and tossed it to Jim Taylor, his fullback.

Bart Starr blocked to the left, and Green Bay halfbacks blocked to the left. The ends blocked to the left. Jim Taylor ran to the left, down the white line at the edge of the field, past the scrimmage line.

The referee watched very carefully to ensure he didn't step out of bounds. Indeed, one of the Browns pointed to the line and complained that Taylor had stopped over the line, but Taylor kept going. He broke one tackle. He broke a second tackle. Jim Taylor might not have been the fastest man in football, but he could be the least stoppable.

The Cleveland Brown linebackers and end zone defenders, who were the fastest on the team, ran to intercept Taylor. Taylor suddenly cut to the right and ran down the middle of the field. A Brown jumped on his back. Taylor threw him off and kept going. One of the Brown ends ran in from the end zone. Taylor straight-armed him, and the guy fell backward. Taylor kept going. The Packers ends ran in from the end zone and ran into the two linebackers blocking for Taylor and fell down. The buzzer signifying the end of time sounded, but Taylor kept going. A slender Cleveland Brown defender tackled Taylor around both ankles. The referee watched closely because if Taylor's forward motion was stopped, time was out, and the game was over. Taylor shook his left foot free and limped, trailing the would-be tackler to the five-yard line. Taylor looked in vain for a Packer close enough to toss the ball to, but he now was going so slowly that the Browns behind him were catching up. Taylor crossed into the end zone and tossed the football underhanded to his coach Vince Lombardi, who was now running onto the field. The referee blew the whistle and raised both arms signifying a touchdown, worth 6 points. The Packers won 12 to 11. Packers fans roared, and noisemakers rattled. The police could no longer keep the cheeseheads off the field. The Browns trooped disconsolately into their dressing room. Some kicked their helmets. The scoreboard flashed several times, Green Bay: 12, Cleveland: 11.

The crowd lifted Lombardi onto their shoulders and danced with him.

The lounge roared. Cal and Ralph hooked elbows and danced around clockwise, then hooked the other elbows and danced around counterclockwise. Soon everyone in the room was dancing and shouting. You'd have thought a bus load of happy Pentecostals had just arrived.

Susanne Carmarthen, the part-time nurse, looked in, laughing. "What happened?"

"Jim Taylor has just made the most fantastic touchdown run in history," Cal yelled. "WE WON!"

Everybody in the room began shouting, "We won! We won!"

Stars twinkled over the bank.

"God be with you, Cal Bedrick. I know the Sienkiewicz family, they are very fine people. You be nice to them, and they'll be nice to you. I have to go intercept a football game in the dining hall. Have a seat until Wilkins comes for you," Mr. Dula said.

* * *

The door to the men's shelter opened. It was Wilkins, wearing a red and black checkered wool hunting jacket. Cal bolted up and hugged Wilkins. Snow was falling outside the open door.

Mr. Dula raised his right hand. Wilkins grinned and raised his right hand. Mr. Dula patted Wilkins on the back.

Cal and Wilkins went outside. It was quite cold. Wilkins hooked his arm to Cal's elbow to support him. They went to the Stone Street Bridge. Cal slipped, but Wilkins caught him before he hit the icy concrete sidewalk. They progressed. The Wisconsin River was black, reflecting the multicolored Christmas ornaments that hung between different sides of Third Street. A Christmas boat played Christmas carols on an electric organ under the bridge. Red and green pendants fluttered. Curious orange clouds formed over Stevens Point far to the south.

They came off the bridge and crossed First Avenue. Wilkins escorted Cal up Stuart Avenue a few paces and turned left past the white propane tanks. Wilkins opened the door. Frannie was there to greet them. Her eyes were moist.

"Oh Cal, I was so worried about you. Come in."

Wilkins looked over the feast table. The kitchen table had been extended by pulling out the leaves. Joey sat in the place of honor underneath the oil portrait of Jesus. On his right, Wendy Gabrilska, Frannie's best friend since grade school, smiled at Wilkins. She waved a hand like a child hoping to be noticed by the teacher. Wilkins politely nodded to Wendy.

Wendy caught eyes with Frannie and mouthed the words *He's gorgeous.*

Into the empty chair on Wendy's right, Frannie and Wilkins gently maneuvered Cal, whose face and hands were bitterly cold. Frannie sat next to Cal on the last chair next to the sink.

Little Brother began putting napkins and silverware at each plate. He sat opposite Cal.

Joey went to the refrigerator and pulled out cans of Polish beer, which he placed in front of each plate except for Wilkins's, who did not drink.

Frannie took out the pork roast and put it on top of the stove, then took a long wooden spoon and dipped it into a saucepan. She dipped out some gravy and held it out to Cal's face.

"Cal, is this gravy sweet enough?"

Cal bent forward and put his mouth around the spoon.

"In my opinion, this is ..."

"Is what?"

"It is ..."

"What, Cal? Speak up."

"As sweet as any pork roast gravy I've ever tasted."

Beaming, Frannie sat the pork roast on the gravy plate and placed it in front of Joey. The wind roared. Snow battered the window behind Joey and the portrait of Jesus. Wilkins brought fresh green beans to the table. Little Brother brought a plate of buttered yams, cut in quarters. They were still steaming, melting the butter very quickly. He sat it down in front of Joey. Frannie felt Cal's forehead. It was definitely cold but not as cold as when he first came in. She told Little Brother to go into the basement and turn up the heating. She brought crispy white bread and a cut glass butter holder to the table. She went back for a green and red salad, which consisted of radishes, red and green lettuce, sliced tomatoes, and beansprouts. This was passed down to Wendy, who turned the salad bowl around so that the wooden salad spoons were there for Joey to serve. Joey served Wendy first and then himself. Wendy passed the bowl down the table to Cal and Frannie and on the other side to Little Brother and Wilkins who had already heaped a pile of buttered yam on his plate.

Wilkins went to the stove. He retrieved steaks of rainbow trout and cooked them two at a time in a grill basket. He roasted one side of the fish, turned it over, and briefly roasted the other side. He put both rainbow trout steaks onto a plate that Frannie held out for him.

Frannie passed the plate to Wendy.

"One for Joey and the other for you," she said to Wendy.

Wilkins was grilling three more rainbow trout steaks. He put the three steaks on a platter. Frannie took the platter. She served it to Little Brother and Cal next to her, and then, with a Sienkiewicz smile, to Wilkins, who stared at it lovingly.

"Where did you get these fish?" Wendy asked.

Frannie jabbed at the air, pointing to Wilkins. "He caught them."

"You caught these?"

"I did, yes, in a trap that the Indians use. They were jumping and going upstream to the north. I caught a few and gave them as a present to Frannie."

"Why a present?"

"Because we all like and admire her."

It was 5 PM and completely black outside. Snow was falling very heavily now. Joey folded his hands together, interlacing the fingers. He turned to the oil portrait of Jesus.

"Dear Lord. We praise you and thank you for this delicious fish that our dear friend Wilkins caught and beautifully cooked. We pray with utmost humility to help our dear brother Cal. He has improved much. Amen," Joey said.

Frannie began to pray.

"Dear Jesus, thank you for helping our brother make it from the men's shelter to our home. These beautiful rainbow trout were cooked by our dear friend Wilkins. We ask you to let your countenance shine upon him."

Cal wobbled upwards. Frannie supported him by holding onto his shoulders.

"We thank the Sienkiewicz family for this lovely meal, and we pray that you thank them in your own blessed way. Thank you."

He sat down awkwardly.

"Thank you, Jesus. Thank you for rescuing our beloved brother Cal. It has been our privilege to follow your example and bring a stranger and a homeless man into our home. In taking care of him, we express our devotion to you, Lord. Amen," Little Brother said.

Joey turned to Wendy.

"Wendy?"

She nodded and stood. She felt uncomfortable among the Catholics. She did not interlace her fingers but simply put her palms together facing the oil portrait.

"We thank you, God, for these wonderful friends and the wonderful food we are about to eat. As soon as our dear friend Frannie remembers to bring the corn on the cob, we will consume that, blessing you all the time."

Frannie gently slapped her forehead, stood, and retrieved the corn on the cob from the stove. She reached for a set of tongs from one of the drawers and used it to transfer the corn on the cob to a pretty Polish ceramic dish that curved up at the ends. She served Joey first. Little Brother made a face.

"Why does he always get served first?"

"He's the boss," Wilkins said.

Joey served Wendy. Everyone took corn on the cob. Frannie held out the cut glass butter holder. Everybody sliced off a good chunk and spread it on their corn on the cob. Wilkins turned off the oven and turned off the burners. Frannie smiled at Wilkins. Wilkins smiled back at Frannie.

Joey poured himself some Polish beer. Little Brother took some too.

"After dessert, whiffle ball," Little Brother said.

Wendy looked confused.

"It's our custom here at the Sienkiewicz house to play three innings of whiffle ball before going to the Christmas mass. You don't have to join us, but you're welcome."

Frannie scooped ice cream and Hershey's chocolate sauce into pewter dishes and put the dishes in front of everybody.

"Oh yummy," Wendy said.

Frannie helped Cal eat the chocolate dessert and so did Little Brother.

They all had some dessert. Wendy licked her lips.

"Any more, Frannie darling?"

Frannie got up, went to the stove and got another pewter dessert dish with a spoon, and reached over Cal. Joey gestured to his pewter cup. Frannie brought over another dessert dish. Little Brother held out his dessert cup as well. Frannie served Little Brother, Wilkins, and herself with a second helping. Wilkins reached out and held Frannie's wrist with a grin.

Cal wobbled at the stove. Wilkins stood quickly, caught him, and put him in his chair. He helped Cal eat his ice cream. Cal slurped the ice cream.

"This is terrific, Frannie."

Cal leaned against Frannie's shoulder. Frannie blushed.

"*Will you marry me*," Cal said in a loud whisper.

"Of course I will, you know I will but not right now, people are watching. We have to talk to Father Leszinski first."

Cal slumped backwards and held Frannie tightly.

"Wilkins, do you know any spiritual dances to help the sick?" Wendy said.

Wilkins thought for a long time.

"Yes, I do."

Gradually they all stood. Wilkins stood and began stomping his feet. Wendy stomped her feet in rhythm to match Wilkins. Wilkins put a hand on Little Brother's shoulder. Little Brother also began to step in time.

Frannie stood and very gently hauled up Cal to his feet.

"Come on darling, this is a spiritual dance, and Wilkins is

leading it. Just step in time and we'll go out into the snow."

Wilkins beckoned for Joey. The two of them led the shuffling step dance.

Little Brother followed them out toward Stuart Avenue.

"Ouch, Joey, you're stomping on my foot," he said.

The trees were bare though covered in snow along the bare branches.

They got to the yellow clapboard house on the corner. A young man with a blond crew cut opened the door. He backed away when he saw Wilkins.

"What are you doing?" he said.

"We are part of a cortege of peaceful members of the neighborhood. We've come to ask you to join us in peace and brotherhood to celebrate the birth of our blessed Lord, Jesus Christ."

"How far are you going?"

"This is as far as we go."

"What's going on, Bill," a young woman's voice said.

"Oh nothing, neighbors making a Christmas call."

"Oh how wonderful."

She came to the door. She was a brunette. Her hair was combed back. She had gold earrings and wore a white blouse. She smiled and held out her hand to be shaken. The entire cortege, one by one, shook her hand.

"Are you a native?" she asked Wilkins.

"Yes ma'am, I am."

"What tribe are you sir," the man with the blond crew cut asked.

"I am Ojibwe."

"But you're not Christian, are you?"

"No ma'am, personally I am not, but many people in my tribe are."

The man with the blond crew cut relaxed with a forced smile. His wife seemed friendlier.

"It was wonderful meeting you fellows but if you'll excuse me I must get back to my baking," the young woman said.

"Yes, it's been a pleasure," the man said.

They went back in and gently closed the door. The wreath jangled.

The cortege danced back to the Jesus house.

They went into the living room.

"Time for whiffle ball," Little Brother said.

Little Brother got out the whiffle ball and bat from behind the door that led to the basement. He had what he needed: A lightweight, airy whiffle ball and a lightweight bat. They all played. Wendy was on Joey's team, so was Wilkins, at first base. That meant Frannie's team, with Cal and Little Brother, were up first. She leveled the bat across a copy of *Newsweek* which was home base.

"Hummer in there, baby, come on, don't be afraid," Frannie said.

But apparently Joey was afraid. He pitched three balls.

"One last chance, Polack."

Frannie walloped Joey's next pitch, over his head where it got tangled in the curtains and on the floor. Wendy couldn't quite pick it up. Finally she did and threw it to Wilkins who bobbled the ball which fell at his feet. He picked it up but Frannie was already going around second base, which was a copy of *Time* magazine. Wendy scooted out of the shadows but Frannie evaded her.

"The ball, Joey, throw the ball to home plate," she said, which he did.

The ball went over Frannie's head. Frannie scampered from third to home plate and made two fists over her head.

"Inside-the-living-room home run!" she declared.

The game continued for three more innings. In the end Wilkins, Joey, and Wendy won 7 to 6.

"Sorry Frannie, I guess I'm out of shape," Cal said.

Frannie patted him gently on the back. "You did fine, Cal, just fine," she said.

"Its 9:30, guys," Joey said. "Let's open our presents."

A bundle of gift-wrapped presents lay on the floor between the red couch and the round marble-topped liquor cabinet. Little Brother picked up one that had his name on it and removed the gift wrapping. It was a framed photograph of the great Henry Aaron.

"Oh my God. Oh, bless you, bless you," Little Brother said. He kissed the gold frame of the photograph of Henry Aaron and hugged it to his breast.

Joey picked up a carefully wrapped package addressed to him. It was also a photograph framed in gold.

"Holy shit, Warren Spahn in mid-wind-up. Who gave this to me?"

"We did," Little Brother and Frannie said in unison.

"Well thank you, thank you from the bottom of my heart."

Joey picked up a second present for himself. It was long, hard, and triangular. He opened it. It was brown laminate with white letters reading "Manager." Joey stared at it.

"How wonderful," he finally said. "Who got me this?"

"It's from Cal," Frannie said, "so your customers will know who to complain to."

Joey laughed and put the desk plaque down. "No complaints yet."

Frannie picked up her beribboned box and opened it. It was a fluffy white bathrobe. She held it up and admired the initials at the bottom: FGS. She put it on.

"Do I or do I not look splendid?" Frannie said.

"Splendid," Little Brother said.

Cal got a gilt-edged New Testament inscribed in front, "Welcome home Cal", signed "Love Frannie".

"Cal, I think there's a bookmark," Frannie said

Cal opened to a bookmark set at the beginning of the Parable of the Prodigal Son. It was the story of a young man who ran away from home, went to the city, and lost all his money gambling. He felt so horrible that he decided to go back home though he had no idea what his father would do to him. His father had aged much, and he walked with a cane, but he stumbled forward and hugged and embraced his long-lost son with all his fading strength.

Cal wiped a tear from his eye. He leaned forward to kiss Frannie on the cheek.

"Uh, ah," Joey broke in.

Cal and Frannie separated and put their arms on each other's shoulders.

It was 11 PM.

"We're going to midnight mass at our church."

"May I come with you?" Cal asked.

Frannie grinned. "Yes, of course."

She grabbed hold of Cal's right forearm. Everybody went to the pantry and got their winter coats. Wendy and Wilkins both left the Jesus house. Wendy hugged Wilkins.

"Hey, that's my coat," Little Brother said.

"You can wear my hunting coat, Little Brother," Frannie said.

Chapter 18

They crossed Third Avenue, where bright Christmas ornaments were swinging in the dying breeze, from Stuart Avenue all the way up to the Big Boy at the south end of Third Avenue.

"Frannie, what would you have said if I had proposed?"

"In fact you did ask, and I did say yes."

There were no lights on in the Hollow. They crossed to Fourth Avenue and turned right past pretty bungalow houses, most of them bright with wreaths on the front door or electric candles in the living room windows. Christmas music played from several of the bungalows. They passed a small stone building. A six-pointed red lamp hung in front of the empty pews.

"That used to be my synagogue," Cal said.

"Nobody's there," Little Brother said.

"Jews don't celebrate Christmas."

"Poor bastards, what do they celebrate?" Joey said.

"Well, there is a holiday called Hanukkah. We light candles, give presents, and eat sweets."

"Well, that's not so bad," Frannie said.

"When is Hanukkah?" Joey asked.

"It varies from year to year, but it's usually around Christmas time. It's a winter lights festival. Lots of cultures have them."

"Well, Christmas is always December 25. It's always steady, steady, steady."

"You know why? The Christians stole the date from the pagan Romans. It was a feast day for the god Saturn."

"That's not true, Cal," Frannie said. "Christmas remained at December 25, even though the solstice was December 21."

They walked on. The neighborhood was dark except for the

porch lights on the pretty bungalow houses. Many had Christmas tree lights on with wrapped presents underneath.

"What about Jesus," Little Brother asked.

"I'm so sorry to tell you this, Little Brother, but Jews don't have a Jesus."

They walked on. There was a small green and red explosion in the middle of the Wisconsin River.

They came to Our Lady of the Holy Sepulcher. It was slightly sunken below snow-covered grass from the sidewalk. The entrance walk had been shoveled and swept. There was a snowman in a priest's cassock and hat to the left of the door. The church was red brick with a large black rosette window behind which candles burned. They went in. It was very cold despite heaters on the floor. The floor was maroon tiles with a wide yellow border with blue fleurs-de-lis. A stunted Norwegian pine Christmas tree stood in the rear corner with a large wood angel on top blowing on a long medieval horn. There was a large crèche on the floor under the Christmas tree with the Virgin Mary, Joseph, and the three magi. Odd-shaped chandeliers hung from the ceiling and gave off a dull gold light, despite which the church was still dark.

"Hey, those lights look like hospital lights," Cal said.

Frannie took Cal's arm in the crook of the left elbow and they walked to the pew.

Green holly with red berries was fixed to the sides of the pews. Tall white candles burned everywhere. They reflected off a stained-glass Gothic window at the rear and shone at the rosette window. They were mounted on a tall black holder of multiple candles that angled up to a peak. Red votive candles were giving off a red glow from black iron rows. The church was surprisingly dark, given all the lights and candles. There was a baptismal basin where they dipped their fingers in Holy Water and made the sign of the cross. There was a door to the rectory, near to which was a confessional booth. An altar was center front, covered in white linen with an upside-down bell and silver platter with white wafers. In front of the altar was a communion rail. A huge crucifix was on the wall behind the altar. There was another stained-glass window above the crucifix. The Crucified One was polychrome, with drops of blood painted on his forehead from the crown of thorns and on his palms and ankles, which were punctured by heavy nails. His head was down, and He was in terrible pain.

By the confessional booth was a small bleacher for the choir, which now filed in wearing white tops and gray bottoms and gray socks and black shoes and carrying songbooks. They took their place in the bleachers.

The church smelled of fragrant wax but also there was an aroma of warm cinnamon and mince from the kitchen below.

Father Leszinski stood at the front of an aisle between rows of pews where people already sat. He wore a white surplice down to his knees, and under it a bright red Christmas cassock down to his bright black shining shoes. He held his hands together, not praying but welcoming. He smiled. He had a beautiful smile and very black hair.

"Merry Christmas, Frannie, Merry Christmas Joey, and Merry Christmas Larry ... Who's this?" he asked, looking at Cal.

"I am Cal Bedrick," Cal said.

"Cal Bedrick," the priest said. "You are always welcome here. This is your church."

"Thank you, Father."

Someone else came into the church. "Merry Christmas, Mrs. Szabo. Merry Christmas, Jerry. Merry Christmas, Richard."

"You can call me Peewee, Father," little Richard said.

The priest laughed.

Another family came in. "Merry Christmas, Terry. Merry Christmas, Mr. and Mrs. Grabow."

"Merry Christmas, Father Leszinski," they said.

Finally everybody was in. The church was not full, but four or five pews were filled. The priest spread his arms to welcome every person.

"Please take a tall white candle from Father Petrus. Let him light it and then pass it one by one to the person on your left so they can light their candle from your flame."

The candle came to Frannie. She looked shyly at Cal, who gently lighted his.

"Welcome to Our Lady of the Holy Sepulcher for our Christmas Midnight Mass. I am Father Leszinski. I recognize most of you. A few of you have just been introduced to me, and in Jesus's name, I welcome you to celebrate the birthday of our Lord."

Suddenly Cal sang,

Happy birthday to you,
happy birthday to you,
happy birthday dear Jesus,
happy birthday to you.

Sister Elizabeth, a roly-poly nun with rimless glasses, polished off "Happy Birthday" with a resounding cadenza on the electric organ in front of the bleachers. She turned to the congregation, most of whom laughed and clapped. Frannie blushed and looked away.

The priest laughed and kept his arms spread. "Everybody may celebrate the birthday of our Lord in any way they wish."

Sister Elizabeth began "O Holy Night." Those who were Catholic stood. Cal sang with Frannie.

O Holy Night, the stars are brightly shining.
It is the eve of our dear Savior's birth.

Frannie looked at him in amazement. "How did you know that song?"

"I went to public school. We all sang Christmas carols."

Fall on your knees, and hear the angels singing,
Oh night divine
Oh night when Christ was born,
Oh night divine
Oh night divine

Most of the congregation sat. Sister Elizabeth played the beginning of "Oh Come Emmanuel," which they sang.

"I will now celebrate the Christmas Mass," Father Leszinski

said softly. "Now, during the mass, you will see me drink a little bit of red wine. This will have been transformed by the power of grace to the actual blood of Jesus Christ." Father Petrus showed the congregation a round wafer which was embossed with the manufacturer's name and "Peoria, Illinois" on a silver platter. "You will also see me swallow this thin white wafer, which has also been transfigured by the power of grace to the actual body of our Lord Jesus Christ," Father Leszinski said. He turned to face the altar.

"What are these pillows on the floor for?" Cal asked Frannie.

"That's so you can kneel," Frannie said.

Father Petrus rang a bell, and everybody except Cal stood, until he felt Frannie's warm hand pulling him up. Father Petrus helped Father Leszinski get down to his knees, facing the altar. Father Leszinski recited a prayer very quietly. Holding a goblet of wine, Father Petrus put it to Father Leszinski's lips. Father Leszinski sipped. Father Petrus delicately wiped Father Leszinski's mouth with a linen cloth and put the goblet back on the altar. Father Petrus took the wafer and gently put it into Father Leszinski's mouth. Father Leszinski prayed quietly and swallowed the wafer. Father Petrus rang the bell again and helped Father Leszinski to his feet. They stood up and turned to the congregation.

"This concludes our Christmas mass. May you go home in peace and live with Jesus." He came forward as though to guide them to the door. "Please help yourself to a Christmas mince pie, cooked in our own kitchen by our own Sister Elizabeth."

The priest went to the doorway, which was now open. Church bells rang all over town. Father Leszinski shook hands with everybody as they filed out, giving them holiday greetings. At the same time, Father Petrus sprinkled sand and salt on the sidewalks.

The priest and Sister Elizabeth held trays with miniature mince pies as they filed out the door. Everybody took one, and shook the priest's hand, wishing him a Merry Christmas.

Cal took one and bit into his mince pie. "Oh boy, this is great. I want to be a Catholic," he said and shook the priest's hand.

"Merry Christmas. No matter where you go and what you do, Jesus is with you," Father Leszinski said.

"Thank you, Father."

Father Leszinski gave Frannie a hug and shook the hands of the rest of the family.

"How I wish your father was here," Father Leszinski said.

"Thank you, Father Leszinski," Cal said

Cal and the Sienkiewiczes went out to Fourth Avenue. The bungalow houses were still brightly lighted with candles, wreaths, and angels. Far away on Third Street, the road was decorated with more Christmas ornaments, including Christmas wreaths and electric candles. Stores on the west side of Third Avenue still had bright illumination. Cal and the Sienkiewiczes crossed Stuart Avenue.

Cal leaned into Frannie's ear and whispered, "I need you, Frannie."

Startled, Frannie stumbled a couple of times when she heard that, and then regained her footing as they crossed Stuart Avenue. They came to the Sienkiewicz house. Cal tried to kiss Frannie on the cheek, but Joey put his hand between Cal's mouth and Frannie's cheek, so Cal kissed Joey's hand instead. "We'll have none of that," Joey said.

"*Thanks for coming to mass Cal*," Frannie whispered. She leaned forward and kissed Cal on the back of the neck.

"Well, time to take our guest home. Come on, Cal," Joey said.

Frannie and Little Brother went inside the house, and Joey and Cal started crossing the Stone Street Bridge, which had a light covering of snow.

"I hope you learned something, Cal," Joey said.

"I did."

On the other side of the bridge was Big Bull Falls, which was mostly whitewater rapids. Down below, the Wisconsin River twinkled with red and green lights from downtown Christmas ornaments and white lights from the bridge. Duck Island was lost in the darkness. Cal looked back once or twice, but Frannie was already inside.

There was a huge explosion in the Wisconsin River by Duck

Island. The explosion was full of a green tint that colored the otherwise black water.

"What the hell was that," Joey said.

"Could be Julius Klein," Cal said. "We used to throw firecrackers into the river just to see what color splash they would make."

"I hope that bastard isn't around here."

They walked on through the snow. It got very quiet.

"Frannie is very nice," Cal said.

"That's why you can't kiss her," Joey said.

"Could I marry Frannie?"

Joey didn't respond. He pressed a white button at the shelter door. To their surprise, Mr. Dula was standing there waiting for them. At the far right just inside the door were presents, donations from the townspeople of Wausau.

"Where have you guys been? It's late."

"I went to Christmas Mass!" Cal said cheerfully.

"At Our Lady of the Holy Sepulcher?"

"Yep."

"That's my church."

Mr. Dula and Joey shook hands. "Merry Christmas," they both said. Joey walked back over the bridge singing "O Holy Night", hitting all the high notes. He stopped on the bridge, leaning against the balustrade. The river was frozen at the shores. A yellow duckling tried to climb a tiny piece of ice floating towards Duck Island, but his slight weight was sufficient to tilt the slab and throw him back into the dark water. He tried again with the same result. He tried a third time and fell into the water. This time he sank.

Mr. Dula opened a cabinet and said, "You can put your clothes in here. They're safe."

Cal did so.

"Mr. Dula, if I marry a Catholic, can I sleep with her?"

"If she's willing, but she may want you to become a Catholic too," Mr. Dula said.

"I'm not willing."

In his sleep, Ralph turned over and said, "Go, Jimmy, go."

Cal got into bed wearing his underwear. Mr. Dula covered him with blankets and then gave him his medicine. Cal swallowed the tranquilizer but refused the anti-depressant.

"Get out of bed and say your prayers."

Cal threw off the covers, jumped out of bed, and got down on his knees with his hands folded against the mattress.

"Get off your knees!"

Cal bolted upright. "Holy shit!"

Mr. Dula was instantly at Cal's side with his hand on Cal's shoulder.

"What the matter Cal? Did you see something?"

"I heard my father."

"Your Heavenly Father?"

"No, my earthly father, the one that's dead."

They sat on the edge of the bed. Mr. Dula stroked Cal's back. "What did your father say?"

Cal's voice trembled. "He told me to get off my knees."

"Why on earth would your father say something like that?"

"Well, he was a Jew, you know, and Jews don't pray on their knees."

"I didn't know that."

"He might also have meant, Don't be a coward, don't convert to Catholicism."

"Cal, I want you to get under the covers again."

Cal got under the covers. Mr. Dula kept his hand on Cal's shoulder. It got very quiet. Tears began forming down Cal's cheeks. Mr. Dula wiped them off with a forefinger.

"Now listen carefully, Cal. I don't want to send you to the psych ward. A lot of people here end up in there."

Cal nodded gratefully

"Touchdown, we won," Ralph said.

Mr. Dula chuckled. He cradled Cal and lay him down on the bed. "Close your eyes, sweetheart," Mr. Dula said. Cal slept.

* * *

The stars were bright over the Sienkiewicz home. Joey went in. It was very comfortable and loving, as it always was after Christmas mass. Frannie served hot chocolate under the portrait of Jesus. They all drank hot chocolate. Joey spoke softly and said, "Frannie, I don't like how you and Bedrick are getting together."

"What on earth do you mean, Joey?"

"You kissed him. Right in front of me!"

"We're 22. We can do that, Joey. It's not like we had sex."

"Purdneer."

"You should talk. You've knocked up Jennifer Wallingford, Julia Munson, and Roberta Gorky."

"I repented. And besides, we're all friends now, and babies were born in all three cases, as the priests tell us sex is for. When I die, I will have no sins on my soul."

Little Brother wrinkled his nose and giggled as he turned to Frannie's face. "Frannie, are you going to have sex with Cal Bedrick?"

Joey wiped off a spoon very carefully, ensuring nothing was on it and bopped Little Brother on the top of the head

"Shush, Little Brother."

Little Brother laughed. "Where were you going to do it, Frannie? On the red couch where Daddy died? Can I watch?"

There was a long silence.

Frannie stood up. "I'm going to bed. I had a wonderful time. Do you mind if I keep the angels going?"

She walked into the living room, pulled out a second stubby white candle, put it under the brass angels, and lighted it. Soon the angels were turning and making a sweet melody.

Frannie went to take a shower. The breeze from outside was cool and refreshing. She looked in vain for the men's shelter, but she crossed herself. She went back to bed without pulling back the covers and smiled.

Downstairs, Joey turned to Little Brother. "I don't like this, Little Brother, not one bit."

Chapter 19

In the morning, when Cal woke, the sun was bright, reflecting through the window, making a cross on Cal's wall. Ralph had gone for breakfast. Cal danced to the dining hall.

After breakfast, Frannie visited Our Lady of the Holy Sepulcher and caught Father Petrus's eye. They went into the confession booth, Frannie on one side, Father Petrus on the other side. They could see each other through gaps in the partition, but not very well. They closed their respective doors.

"How can I help you?" Father Petrus asked.

"I have sinned, Father."

"How have you sinned, my child?"

"I have had impure thoughts."

"Concerning what have you had impure thoughts?"

"I am taking care of a homeless man."

"That is no sin, my child. Indeed, that is your Christian duty."

"I have begun to like him."

"Do you like him too much? Is that why you call it a sin?"

"Yes."

"Is he married?"

"No."

"Do you want sex with him?"

"Yes."

"That is a very cardinal sin. Have you prayed to the Holy Mother?"

"Many times."

"What have you prayed for?"

"For her to protect the man."

"From whom?"

"From the cold . . . and from me."

"Where is he now?"

"He is in the men's shelter."

"Do you see him often?"

There was a pause.

"Sometimes."

"Pray to the Holy Mother of God to release you from the obsession. Nothing you have said is correct unless you two marry."

"Thank you, Father Petrus."

There was a long pause

"This type of obsession can spread. Pray to the Holy Mother to rid you from these impure thoughts and read the New Testament. Come back to confession in a week. See if you feel freer."

"Yes, I will. Thank you, Father Petrus."

"Go, and sin no more."

Frannie stood and pushed open her door. She left the church.

Frannie went from the church to the men's shelter. She went in and waved to Mr. Dula.

"Is Cal Bedrick here?"

"I'll bring him to you," Mr. Dula said.

Mr. Dula went to the three-bed dorm. Cal sat up. Mr. Dula helped him put on the shelter pajamas and slippers. Cal shuffled into the lobby.

"Hi, Cal."

"Oh, Frannie, how nice to see you. I really enjoyed Christmas mass."

"So did I. I made a reservation for us for New Year's Eve at the Moose in the Woods. It's just around the corner. They always have a special do on New Year's Eve."

"Should I come to pick you up?"

"No, I'll pick you up, and we'll walk back over the Stone Street Bridge together. Wear your new clothes, Cal, the ones that Ralph has gotten for you from Brooks Men's Clothiers. The Piggly Wiggly will be closed."

Chapter 20

On December 31, the shelter served eggnog and pastries after 9:30 PM. Frannie came to pick Cal up, and they walked together, with hooked arms, down the Stone Street Bridge and turned left onto Third Avenue and went into the Moose in the Woods restaurant. Outside, there were big dogs and little dogs. Many of them had fake antlers on their foreheads. The light above was yellowish brown. Next door was the Wausau Gun and Tackle store. Cal peered in. Racks of rifles and shotguns lined the rear wall behind the counter. They sold fishing licenses and hunting licenses, sportsmen's floppy brimmed hats with a band to hold fishhooks, and a whole counter of fish lures.

"I remember this store. The owner was very nice. He would refer fishermen to me. I used to dig up black earth with earthworms, put them in a box, and keep them in our garage. A quarter for a dozen if I recall. I got rich!"

"Well, you see Cal, you were an entrepreneur," Frannie said. "Don't forget that."

They went into the restaurant. Frannie pointed to the mistletoe. "You know what that's for, Cal?"

"Yep, somebody gets to kiss somebody."

"Well, who will it be?"

"Well, if you don't mind," he leaned forward and gave Frannie a smooch on the cheek.

Just then, a waitress wearing antlers came up.

"Bedrick, party of two," Frannie said.

"Right this way."

She sat them in a booth facing each other, under a moose head on the wall.

"Would you two like to start with a rum eggnog?" the waitress asked.

"Make it double strong," Cal said.

"What about you, ma'am?" the waitress asked.

"No, no rum for me, just eggnog," Frannie said.

"I'll bring a menu," the waitress said, then walked away.

Although it was cold outside, it was warm and even stuffy inside, as people were celebrating New Year's.

An aquarium on the wall displayed yellow and black swordtail fish and white angelfish. There was a marble castle at the base and undulating green lake weeds. There were giant posters of the North Woods.

The restaurant was packed. Frannie's eyes kept darting to the opposite wall. Two veterans sat there with cheeseburgers. They were not Fitz and Rafe. She relaxed.

A toddler went to the aquarium, lay on the floor underneath, and slept.

The waitress brought their eggnog, which they raised and hooked elbows so they could drink out of the glass held by the other.

"Happy New Year!"

"Happy New Year!"

Cal drank his in one gulp. Frannie frowned and daintily drank from hers. Cal folded his hands and put them on the table.

"I used to have a little red wagon. I went from door to door in the neighborhood collecting old newspapers." Cal said. "When my wagon was full, my mom and I tied them into squares and put them in the trunk of her Chevy, and then she drove the papers and me out to the truck weighing station at the edge of town. We drove out onto the scale, which was a platform. They weighed us with the newspapers, then took out all the newspapers, weighed us again, figured out the difference, and paid us accordingly."

"Wow, you really *were* an entrepreneur. I'd hire you anyway."

"I used to earn $10! My mom was so proud of me. It was my idea, you know."

The waitress brought their menus.

"What do you recommend?" Cal asked.

"The fish is delicious, and so is the venison."

"I'd like the salmon dinner, please, and another eggnog, double rum," he said to the waitress.

"For you, ma'am?"

"Pork roast and dumplings, please."

"Can I get you another eggnog?" the waitress asked.

Frannie shook her head.

"Cal, I didn't know you drank alcohol."

"Well, it's New Year's Eve."

There was a clock with Roman numerals behind the counter. It was 11:20. Cal drained the second eggnog.

Headlight beams came through the windows. The chef was visibly very busy behind the counter. Cal looked at the posters of a forest deep in snow.

"I've been told that cross-country skiing in the winter through the forest when it's utterly quiet is the most heavenly experience," Cal said.

"I've never done it, but it sounds good," Frannie replied.

Their dinner was served. The waitress noticed Cal's empty glass.

"Another, sir?"

"Yes please," Cal slurred.

The waitress left. She came back with another eggnog.

"Is this double rum?" he asked.

"Yes sir," the waitress replied.

"Cal, this is your third one. How are you going to get home?" Frannie said.

"Leaning on your shoulder."

They ate.

"This pork roast could be Polish. It's excellent."

"The salmon is so tender, wow."

Cal stole one of Frannie's dumplings and finished his scalloped potatoes. It was 11:30. The waitress came and took the plates away.

"How was dinner?"

"Marvelous."

"All I require is another double —"

"No Cal, you've had enough."

"Well, I'm going to have another. It's New Year's Eve, darling. If you don't like it, sit and watch."

"I'll be right back with another eggnog for you," the waitress said hesitantly.

"Double rum."

"I know."

Cal looked up to his right. There was a large moose head with enormous antlers.

"I don't think I like this guy watching me."

"It's a moose."

Cal leaned forward. "I'm a bit under the weather. Did you say mouse?"

"No, moose."

The waitress brought another eggnog and put it in front of Cal. "Sorry, did you say mouse?"

"No, *mooooose*!"

Cal drank. Put the glass down. "Why would anybody put a moose on the wall?"

The vets were listening with smiles.

"It's a trophy."

Cal finished his eggnog. "Of what?"

"Of killing a moose."

"Why would you want to kill a moose?"

"To get a trophy on a wall."

"Have you ever shot a moose?"

"Yes."

"Where?"

"The North Woods Lake District of northern Wisconsin," Frannie said.

"Was he going to eat you?"

"Oh no, he was eating water plants."

"And what exactly was this moose doing that was so obnoxious that you had to end its existence?"

"You've never hunted, have you Cal? You've missed a wonderful thing."

Frannie pulled a sheet of paper out of her purse.

Outside, a German shepherd went by with antlers affixed to its forehead. Frannie folded her arms and leaned over a little bit to Cal. Her eyes were sparkling green. She raised the pen.

"How many children do you want?" she asked Cal.

Cal looked at the waitress, raised his empty eggnog glass, and tapped on it.

"No, you've had enough."

"I need one more double to get through this."

"First, tell me how many children you want."

"I don't know. I hadn't thought about it."

"Well, now's the time to think about it."

"One, maybe two."

"I was thinking more like six or seven."

"Well, I guess."

Frannie wrote down "six or seven".

"Do you promise to bring them up Catholic?" she asked.

"No."

She put down the pen "Cal! I am a Catholic."

"I'm not."

"Well, I think you should be, don't you?"

"No, I have no religion."

"What about the children?"

"Oh yes, that's fine."

Frannie wrote down "Mass: every Sunday."

"For the children," Cal said.

"We can talk about it. They will all study the Catechism, won't they?"

"I don't know what a Catechism is," Cal said

"It's a summary of the faith for children," Frannie said. She continued down the list, "And they'll have their first communion at their seventh birthday?"

"They can have their tenth by then. I don't care."

"Cal, this is serious."

"Okay, okay, they can have their first communion at seven."

"And you'll keep on working at the Piggly Wiggly?"

"If your brother doesn't fire me."

Frannie brightened.

Cal finished his eggnog and fell onto his knees out of his booth seat. The two vets watched what he would do next. Cal reached out his left arm until it landed on Frannie's shoulder.

"FRANNIE SIENKIEWICZ!"

"Not so loud Cal."

"WILL YOU DO ME THE HONOR..."

"Go Cal go," one of the vets said.

"... OF MARRYING ME AND BECOMING MY WIFE?"

"Yes Cal, I will."

The vets applauded. On his hands and knees, Cal crawled over to the bigger of the two vets.

"Can I trouble you to get me back on my booth seat?"

The two vets pulled him to his booth, and sat him on his cushioned seat facing Frannie.

"Cal, if you ever need to have somebody testify that you were pissed drunk when you proposed, we'll speak for you."

Cal snored.

Horns began to beep outside. Firecrackers went off. It was midnight. Frannie put her sheet of paper back in her purse. Inside, party horns unrolled and whistled.

People got up to dance. The vets stumbled over to Frannie and politely asked, "Can we possibly have a dance? Your fiancé is out cold in his booth."

Frannie laughed. "Yes, of course."

She got up, held out her hand, and began to dance with one of the vets. By the time they circled the floor, Frannie had taken the other vet by the hand and danced with him. People were singing "Auld Lang Syne," and Frannie joined in. The movement around the restaurant stopped while they sang. Cal stirred. He sat on the edge of the booth seat, unsure of what was going on.

"Who is singing what?" he said.

The waitresses went from table to table, holding a sprig of mistletoe over their heads. They were kissed plenty.

Frannie danced with the second vet until she got to Cal. She held out her hand.

"Up, my pumpkin."

Cal stood. He suddenly sat. He blinked his eyes a lot. Gradually customers filed out, some very happy, some very sober, some very not so. The waitress with the antlers escorted Cal to the door.

The waitress opened the door with mistletoe.

"Do I get to kiss you now?"

"Well, she's your fiancée now, so you should kiss her."

Cal kissed the waitress on the lips.

"Oh wow sir, that was above and beyond the call of duty."

"Cal Bedrick, my love, I am here."

Cal turned around and kissed Frannie on the lips.

"Wow, you girls have kisses sweeter than wine."

"Can you carry him home?"

They were on the sidewalk, dodging dogs with antlers on their foreheads. Cal turned around and banged the back of his head into a lamp post.

"For heaven's sakes Cal, look where you're going."

"I can't go where I'm looking."

She took him by the arm and led him down Third Street past the Moose in the Woods and around the corner. He kept stumbling. She kept holding onto him. When they got to the Jesus house, Frannie opened the kitchen door. They could see Joey and Little Brother inside nursing an eggnog each. Cal grabbed Frannie and kissed her on the lips. Blushing, she let him into the kitchen, where Joey and Little Brother were already sitting. Two glasses of eggnog stood in front of them.

Cal tried to kiss Frannie on the lips again.

"Cal, my whole family is watching."

"Well, I'll kiss them too."

They went in. Frannie had Cal by the crook of the elbow. He fell more than sat in a chair at the kitchen table and then fainted onto the kitchen floor.

"Bring lover boy some strong black coffee, Frannie," Joey said.

Cal was asleep.

Chapter 21

On January 3, an arctic wind blew down over the Canadian plains into Wisconsin. It was bitterly cold. It was minus thirty-five degrees Fahrenheit and minus fifty in the cranberry bogs. Elementary schools were closed. The tots were all bundled up in quilted winter outfits and trousers. You couldn't tell male from female. The weather stick over the bank was all green, meaning colder tomorrow. The top red light was flashing, indicating snow.

A young girl named Mary Jo Tomahawk was caught trying to steal a wallet and socks from Sippl's Department Store just across a narrow alley from the Szabos' tenement.

They caught her, slapped her, retrieved the items, and threw her out of the store, warning her never to come back, but she did.

At twilight, when the light was dark indigo, she sneaked into the store and into the lady's room with a box of wooden matches. She stuffed a wad of paper towels into a basket and dropped in a lighted match. Soon the flames became visible. She backed up to the door, very pleased. A yellow wall began to char, and the char crept upwards towards the ceiling. She got scared and opened the door to leave. The fresh air coming in from the open door blew the flames higher, and the charring went on more rapidly until it was bumping against the ceiling. She let the door close and ran out. Mary Jo Tomahawk watched Sippl's from across the street. Smoke was issuing from the basement window. There was a commotion inside the store.

Mr. Sippl, in a white shirt and maroon tie, ushered customers out of the building. He ordered staff of the new shift to carry down everything they could from the second and third floors, especially the mink and fur coats, which they did. Mr. Sippl ran back in and ran out carrying a heavy cash register and the box of daily receipts. He put these in the trunk of his car, which he locked, making sure that nobody could really see him, then ran back to urge on the fire trucks.

"Hurry! Hurry! There are shirts on the fourth floor worth a fortune. They're not all insured," he cried.

When the first fire engine came, flames were visible in the first-floor windows. The firemen screwed huge brass hose couplings to the fire hydrants, opened the plugs with a wrench, and poured the water into the basement through the broken windows. Now smoke began to issue from the second floor. The second fire truck arrived. A policeman stopped Mr. Sippl from running up to the first or second floors.

"But that's the furniture!" he yelled hysterically.

A second policeman came to hold him back and push him across the street, where he watched flames starting to lick out of the windows of the second floor, which had crashed open.

"Hurry up! Hurry up!" Mr. Sippl yelled.

The crowd was now very large. Some of them helped him move his furniture across the road, where Mary Jo still watched.

The fire chief arrived in a patrol car and ordered one team of hose men to arch their water onto the roof, which was smoking as sparks were rising high. Sparks floated over the yellow pebble aluminum cladding of the Szabos' tenement and even beyond that, as far as Cal's old two-family house.

Mrs. Szabo ran down the stairs with a Thermos of hot coffee for the fire chief.

On West Street, under a stiff and clacking tree with bare branches, a blue and green car was parked, not that new. A young couple embraced in the front seat. The girl was blonde and wore a blue dress with green lily patterns. She sat behind the steering wheel. She pivoted into the passenger seat and straddled the man, humping. Sparks flew over the car.

By the morning, there was nothing left of Sippl's except huge spires, sheets, and domes of hard ice that covered what had been the internal circular stairwells, counters, and two doorframes. Stalagmites punctured the broken bricks. The firemen stayed away from the one remaining wall where enormous stalactites fell without warning and met their own shadows on the ice below with a lethal crash. The drug store was smoking. Police guarded the door. Firemen chipped away at the wall between Sippl's and Schwarzkopf's pharmacy. The pharmacist filled bags with medications, and carried them outside in his arms. The roof fell in. In the morning, Peewee, Jerry, and everyone in the neighborhood stood behind the policemen's yellow tape. Firemen chopped where smoke was still rising.

Some papers from the drug store floated out and twirled softly and gently to the ground.

The firemen would not leave for another few hours, until all the embers were out. The floors of Sippl's had fallen. Gutters of water had frozen all over West Street and Third Avenue, where traffic was still blocked by the police. All the goods were destroyed except the few that Mr. Sippl had managed to push across Third Avenue. Mr. Sippl was not insured.

The temperature reached minus fifty-five in the cranberry bogs. The smoke pots were doing their best to warm up the cranberry plants. Mr. Dula had expelled Fitz and Rafe. They tried to warm themselves up by lighting fires in the thrown-away naphtha pile outside the dry cleaners, but it didn't work. By 3 PM, they had frozen to death, their arms around one another.

Chapter 22

It was February 14 and deathly cold. A flatbed truck with chained-down stripped logs and a red cloth fluttering at the rear rumbled across the bridge.

The Piggy Wiggly was packed with guilty husbands and lovers looking for something last-minute for Valentine's Day. Joey gave Cal a bunch of orange roses and a beautiful box of Piggly Wiggly chocolate, all wrapped up with brown ribbon.

"It's Valentine's Day, *Dummkopf.* Take these to your intended. You know where she is. Can you get there?"

"Yeah, I think I can make it."

"Get down on one knee and say the following with as much sincerity as you can: 'Frannie, I love you. Let's get married. I can't wait.' You try it."

"I love you, Frannie. Let's get married right away."

"With more feeling, for heaven's sake. You do like her, don't you? What are you wasting your life for?"

Cal tottered down Third Avenue on shaky feet toward the Moose in the Woods. He turned the corner onto the long green lawn parallel to Stuart and the Sienkiewicz home, holding out the Valentine's Day gifts like beacons. Frannie was in the kitchen, putting something in the oven: a heart-shaped chocolate pie. Cal knocked on the kitchen door. Frannie opened it. He held out the roses and chocolates.

"Why Cal, how sweet of you."

Cal's eyes were impaired, but he managed to look her in the eyes and say, "Frannie, I love you. Let's get married. I don't want to waste my life."

"Welcome, Sir Galahad. It's so nice to hear that from you. Especially without any eggnog in you. Of course I'll marry you.

You always knew that."

"Can we kiss on the lips now?"

"No, not in front of Jesus."

"He's not looking. He doesn't mind."

"He is always watching in this house."

Cal struggled to his feet.

"I don't care," he said, then grabbed Frannie and kissed her fervently on the lips.

The door opened. Little Brother came in and pointed to them both.

"SIN! SIN! YOU BOTH ARE IN THE STATE OF SIN!"

Cal and Frannie let go of each other instantly.

"We're not doing nothing, Little Brother."

"Oh yes you are, and right in front of God."

Little Brother ran into the pantry. He unzipped the rifle casing. Frannie ran in and zipped it back up.

"What are you doing, Little Brother!" she yelled.

"This is a house of Jesus."

They fought for the rifle.

"Help me, Cal!"

Cal went clumsily into the pantry and, with Frannie's help, yanked the rifle by the barrel out of Little Brother's hands just as Joey opened the kitchen door and came in.

"What the hell is this? Are you going to shoot my bellybutton or something?"

"Little Brother threatened us."

"Why in the hell would he do that?"

"They were kissing! On the lips! In front of God!" Little Brother said, pointing to the portrait of Jesus.

"Is that true, Frannie?"

Frannie blushed. "Yes, it's all my fault."

"Well, let's sit down at the kitchen table and talk it over with Jesus," Joey said.

They all sat at the kitchen table.

"How long have you been doing this?" Joey asked

"We did it under the mistletoe at Moose in the Woods. Cal asked, and I could not resist. You understand, Joey."

"Of course I do, but it's a sin."

"Well, he had just proposed, and I had said yes."

"Is that true Cal?"

"As far as I'm concerned, we're married."

"Not as far as God is concerned. That doesn't happen until the wedding, ain't that right, Frannie."

She nodded sheepishly. "Yes, that's right."

Joey stared at Frannie. "Have you spoken to the priest?"

"We will. I made an appointment with Father Leszinski."

Chapter 23

The next morning, Cal woke.

"Sit up darling," Frannie said.

Cal did not quite realize where he was, but he sat up and put his legs over the edge of his bed. Frannie put his clothes on the bed.

"Get dressed. We're going to see Father Leszinski."

"Oh, I liked him. Why are we going there?"

"To talk about our marriage."

"Are we getting married?"

"That's what you said last night. Have you changed your mind?"

Cal reached out and held both of Frannie's hands. "If you're still willing?"

"I am. I am willing. I am more than willing."

She helped him dress in his new clothes from Ralph. Together, they went to the church, Our Lady of the Holy Sepulcher. The snow was ankle deep except the walkway to the church door which had been shoveled, sanded, and salted. Inside the church, a woman in a kerchief on hands and knees was washing the floor with a sponge, out of a bucket of water. No one else was in. Frannie crossed herself as she passed the huge polychrome wooden crucifix behind the altar. Cal feebly followed her example.

Frannie and Cal met Father Leszinski in the study to discuss the wedding. Father Leszinski folded his hands in front of his stomach. He had been gaining weight. He beamed at Frannie.

"I baptized you so many years ago," he said.

"Yes, you did," she grinned.

"And now, Frances Sienkiewicz, you want to marry this character."

"I do."

"Do you love him?"

"Yes."

The priest raised his eyebrows and turned to Cal. "There's no divorce in the Catholic faith. Do you understand that, Cal? Once you say, 'I do,' you're hooked."

"Yes sir," Cal said.

"Yes Father," Frannie corrected.

"Yes Father," Cal said.

"And adultery is a sin, Cal," Father Leszinski said.

"I don't even know anyone else."

"Even the woman next door, you must not covet her," Father Leszinski said. "You're marrying a wonderful girl. She will take care of you and protect you."

There was a long pause.

"Did you want to ask me a question?" Father Leszinski said to Cal.

Cal stirred uncomfortably.

"Well, don't hold your peace in here. There are no secrets from Jesus."

There was another pause.

"The New Testament begins, 'In the beginning was the Word.' *Word* is capitalized in the New Testament, but that's not correct. It should begin 'In the beginning, God created the heavens and the earth' and go on from there. Also, the Bible moved the book of Isaiah right near the end of the Old Testament so it leads somewhat naturally to the presentation of Jesus. But there is no Jesus, of course, in the Old Testament."

Father Leszinski smiled.

"I can guess what faith you held before your intention to marry this wonderful girl."

Cal stirred again.

"Well, it's a commonly asked question, of course. The answer is that the New Testament is not a sequel to the Old. Some things are based on it, of course, but we believe in the New Testament, just as you once believed in the Old Testament, which carefully excised any reference to Jesus."

"After Job rebukes God, God never speaks in the Old Testament."

"No, he seems to become somewhat contrived."

Frannie was getting uncomfortable.

"I didn't know you knew the New Testament that well," Frannie said.

"I read it every night you thought I was sleeping. If you take out Jesus and the miracles, it's a wonderful book."

"You never told me all of this."

"You never asked, Frannie."

"Are the two of you absolutely determined to get married?"

"Yes," Frannie said, but she sounded confused.

Father Leszinski turned to Cal.

"Will you marry Frances as a Catholic or as a non-Catholic?"

"Can you marry a Catholic to a non-Catholic?"

"Yes, we've done it several times. But you would have to exchange vows during a mass which we call the Nuptial Mass. It's part of the acceptance of Christ by you. You would also have to give an undertaking that your children would be raised as Catholic and that you would participate in the teaching of the Catechism."

Cal turned to Frannie. He looked bewildered.

"Do I have to do all of this?" he asked Frannie.

"If you want to marry me, Cal."

Cal looked back at Father Leszinski, who was studying him closely.

"Are you willing to do this, Cal?"

Cal felt Frannie's hand squeeze his.

"Yes," he said weakly.

Frannie sighed a sigh of relief.

"How many children will you have?" the priest asked after a while.

Frannie and Cal look at each other.

"Let's have three kids, like your family," Cal said. Frannie nodded. "At least," she said.

"Where will you live?" the priest asked.

Cal turned to Frannie. "I'd love to have a home. First, we can live in your house, can't we?" She nodded slowly. "Until the kids are no longer with us," she said.

"Are you earning any money?" the priest asked Cal.

"I'm proud to say that I work part-time at the Piggy Wiggly. Joey is teaching me."

"Joey Sienkiewicz is very competent," the priest said.

There was another pause.

"Have you ever had sex?" Cal asked.

The priest turned red, and Frannie playfully slapped Cal on the knee. "Cal!"

"Before I was a priest."

"With a man or a woman?"

Father Leszinski looked over at Frannie. "Frannie, are you sure you want to marry this guy?"

"I'm not quite so sure now, but yes."

"You have to know in your heart that God wants you to do this."

"I'm sure, as I am sure that Jesus is right for me."

"Well, Father?"

"Before I was a priest, I had a very close attachment to a male friend. We still write to one another, but that's all."

"Thank you for being honest, Father," Cal said.

"We all must be honest. Just one more thing," the priest said. He reached into his drawer. He pulled a nude female doll and a nude male doll without genitals. He demonstrated as he explained. "The proper method of intercourse is as follows. The woman lies on her back. She spreads her legs." The priest spread the female doll's legs. Frannie blushed. The priest put the male doll on top of the female. "The man gets on top of her. He should have an erection by this time. He goes in and out. Sperm comes out from him, and a baby is born. That is the only purpose of sexual intercourse. Is that understood?"

They were both blushing now. They both nodded. Father Leszinski put the dolls back and closed the drawer.

"And Cal, you must accept Jesus Christ as your personal savior, believe in Him, and trust Him."

"I'll do what I can, Father," Cal said.

"He's a good lad," Frannie said.

"Well, it's forever, Frannie, you know that don't you?"

"Yes."

Father Leszinski took an appointment book from the top of the desk and paged through it. "We should have a rehearsal for the wedding ceremony. How about March 18?"

"That would be fine," Frannie said.

"Cal, no objection?" the priest asked.

"It might be cold," Cal said.

"Well, it's only a rehearsal. The wedding itself will be on March 20, the first day of spring. There will be crocuses, tulips, apple blossoms, and birds singing all over Duck Island. It will be beautiful."

Frannie laughed in sheer joy, then squeezed Cal's left hand in both of hers. "I'm so excited!"

"Did you want to ask me anything else?" the priest said, looking at Cal.

Cal shook his head. They stood and shook the priest's hand.

"Come closer so I may bless you."

They came forward and lowered their heads. Father Leszinski put his hands on their heads.

"May the Lord Jesus Christ bless you and keep you. May he strengthen you in your faith. May Jesus make His countenance shine upon you and your children."

They hugged the priest and went to the door. Frannie turned and waved to the priest.

"Cal, you are the strangest person I've ever met," Frannie said.

"No, I'm the strangest one you will ever marry."

They walked through the church toward the door. The woman was finished sponging off the floor. Frannie crossed herself as she passed by the polychrome Christ. She nudged Cal on the ribs. He slowly crossed himself. They walked out. The air was frigid.

"What shall we do now?" Frannie asked.

"Well, there's an exhibit of duck painters at the Yawkey Museum I'd like to go to," Cal said.

"Excuse me?"

"Art clears my head."

"But then you'll come back to the Jesus house."

"Yes."

"Promise."

"What? Sure, I promise."

They hugged. Frannie went to the Jesus house. Cal went to the Yawkey Museum.

* * *

It was dark by the time Cal returned to the Jesus house. Frannie's red hair was precisely curled. He grinned. He tussled her hair. Frannie nursed a strong coffee from a cute European-style demitasse.

"Oh, the smell is wonderful, could I have some?"

Frannie pointed to the percolator. Cal stood, went to the percolator, made some strong coffee, and poured it into another European-style demitasse, the kind they both loved.

"Well," Frannie said.

"Well, I met a lot of painters who were very proud of their work. They were disconsolate, though, that the art world did not take them seriously."

"No, I meant what are your thoughts about Father Leszinski."

"Oh, he's a bastard like all priests, but he seemed nice enough," Cal answered very quickly.

"Don't you ever call him a bastard or a fascist or anything like that. He's helped our families through so many crises I couldn't tell you."

"Sorry."

Cal sipped his coffee carefully.

"It occurred to me that he's like a debater. He's been primed to answer all the questions, especially from anti-Catholics, or new Catholics. I wouldn't have a chance with him."

"Why would you want to argue with the priest that's going to marry you to me?"

Cal took another cup of coffee.

"Just speaking my mind. You know Frannie, we should probably talk about our respective religions so we know each other completely."

"I agree."

"Are there any coffee biscuits?"

Frannie pointed to the coffee pot on the counter. Cal went over and got some coffee biscuits and brought them to the table along with more very hot coffee.

"I need to think about some things," Cal said. He got up, munching on a biscuit. "Back soon," he said with his mouth full.

He went out and walked across several roads bypassing the Jesus house and went down the one remaining path onto Duck Island. It was cold. A few silver droplets hit Cal. There was a duck painter with a standup easel. Cal went over to look.

"*That's very good,*" Cal whispered.

The duck painter raised his left hand.

"*Shhh.*"

"Sorry, I didn't mean to interrupt."

Once again the painter held up his left hand.

"*SHHH!*"

Cal walked across Duck Island. The ground was snowy and spongy. He went to the place where he had first slept after coming back from Stevens Point. It was at the north end. There was an eerie orange glow from the south of the river. Cal closed his eyes but could not evade the damp fragrance of the mud and snow.

He got up slowly and walked back to the Jesus house. He walked in and hung up his winter coat. He sat down by Frannie, who was still on her second cup of coffee.

"Well, sure, Frannie, if you want me to be a Catholic I'll be a Catholic. What's more important now?"

* * *

That night Joey served Polish sausage, pierogi, and Polish beer. They ate.

"Joey, I've been so grateful for all the help you've given us after

Mum and Dad died and how beautifully you've maintained the home," Frannie said.

"He's very handy," Little Brother said.

"But I'm 23 years old and would like to manage my own life," Frannie said. "We've always been a happy family, haven't we?"

"Yup," Joey said and then drank a little more beer.

"And we're a happy family now, aren't we?" Frannie said.

"Yep."

"And we will always be a happy family no matter what comes our way, won't we, Joey?"

There was a long pause. Joey finished drinking from his can and glared suspiciously at Frannie. He didn't say anything for a while, then finally said, "Yes Frannie, we will always be a happy family," with a strange look in his eyes.

Frannie went to the refrigerator, opened a second can of Polish beer, and handed it to Joey, who slowly crumpled the first can in his powerful right hand. He drank from the second can and put it down carefully.

"No matter who or what comes our way?" she said.

"When will something come our way Frannie?"

"March 20."

"What happens on March 20?" Little Brother asked.

"I will walk our sister down the aisle," Joey said.

Chapter 24

That night Frannie could not sleep. She called her best friend, Wendy Gabrilska, whose father taught girls' volleyball and girls' basketball at the high school.

"Hello?" a sleepy Wendy said.

"It's Frannie."

"I know it is. Do you have any idea what time it is?"

"I reckon it's about 3 in the morning."

"Actually, it's 2:45. What's the problem?"

"I need a wedding dress."

"Well, you can't wear mine. That would be bad luck. Who the hell are you marrying?"

"Cal Bedrick."

There was a long, long pause.

"Do you know what you're doing, Frannie?"

Frannie was getting slightly hysterical.

"No, I don't. I need you by my side. Please."

"Well, I'm not a Catholic, as you know, but we've been friends since third grade."

"Do you still have your wedding gown catalogs?" Frannie asked.

"Yes, I can bring them over."

"That would be a blessing," Frannie said.

"Cal mustn't see the gowns that we're looking at. That would also be bad luck. I'll be over tomorrow, but not real early."

Wendy hung up. Frannie lay back, closed her eyes, and looked at the photograph of the Pope on her dresser.

"Get me through this, Your Holiness. That's all I ask, and I pray I don't make a mistake."

The next morning, Wendy knocked at the door. Frannie opened it. Wendy glared at Frannie.

"Are you sure about this?"

"Yes."

They embraced. Wendy was crying a little bit.

"You're not supposed to do that until we say 'I do.' "

"I've known you since you rescued me from Bobby Telmer at the fence."

"Make some coffee, sweetheart, or shall I make it for you?" Wendy said.

"You make it for me, please," Frannie said.

Frannie sat down at her customary chair, which was at right angles to the Jesus portrait. Wendy boiled some water, made some very strong coffee, and got down two very pretty coffee mugs with Mexican folklore designs from a cabinet.

Wendy pulled out a stack of wedding catalogs from a canvas bag. She set the stack on a chair next to her.

"Good Lord Wendy, you sure did your research."

"Yes, I did, for all that it mattered."

Wendy folded her hands on the table.

"So, this Bedrick business. Did he actually propose?"

"Yes, he did."

"And you didn't, God help us, say yes."

"God did help me," Frannie said, "and yes, I did say yes."

"What had gotten into you?"

Frannie drank from her coffee cup.

"Do you want some milk or cream?"

"No, just black. The way the Good Lord made it."

"Where are Cal and Joey right now?" Wendy asked.

"They're both at the Piggly Wiggly. Joey agreed to hire Cal as an assistant."

"Well, that's a relief," Wendy said. "Do you think Cal can keep the job?"

"I'll bash him if he doesn't, and he knows it."

"What about Wilkins?"

"He's out of the picture," Frannie said.

Wendy finished her coffee and dabbed at her mouth with a fresh white napkin that Frannie had put on the table. Frannie carefully took Wendy's empty coffee cup and put it on the kitchen counter.

"Please, could I have some more, Frannie dear?"

Frannie poured black coffee into Wendy's coffee cup and brought the cup back to Wendy. Wendy grabbed a stack of wedding catalogs from the chair and placed them on the kitchen table.

"Well, can we begin?" Frannie said.

Frannie opened the top catalog and paged through the wedding gowns.

"They don't light my fire," Wendy said.

"Me neither," Frannie said.

"Next."

Frannie opened the next catalog. It was dog-eared at the wedding gown section. They both studied the white gowns in their bewildering array. Frannie put her finger on one gown.

"Maybe?" Wendy said, looking at Frannie.

"Well, maybe. Let's keep going."

They went through the entire pile of seven catalogs and only came up with three possibilities.

"You know what I think," Wendy said, "We should walk over to Gowns by Carole to see what she has."

"Good idea. Let's put on our winter coats. Off we go."

They went out the kitchen door and passed the white propane tanks.

"Where's Little Brother?"

"He doesn't want anything to do with this. He thinks *he's* going to marry me."

"You have an interesting family, Frannie."

"He just won't accept it. He's partly insane, you know, and partly a moron on certain topics, like this one."

They crossed the Stone Street Bridge. They passed the men's shelter and turned the corner past the Hotel Wausau. The weather stick on the bank was totally green, and the top red light was not blinking.

“Colder, but no snow tomorrow,” Wendy said.

“Oh, that’s good,” Frannie said.

They turned the corner and went into Gowns by Carole.

Carole was a statuesque woman with light brown hair. Her hands were folded together.

“Sooner or later, all prospective brides come to Carole. I see you’ve got some catalogs. Can I see what you’ve picked so far?”

Frannie opened the catalogs to the dog-eared pages.

“Your taste does not run to the conventional.”

“Is that a problem?” Frannie said.

“It depends on who makes the wedding gown.”

“Do you make them here?”

“Can do, but sometimes I order them from a woman I’ve known for years in West Allis,” Carole said, “Well, come, try on what I do have.”

Wendy and Frannie followed Carole to a rack at the back of the store. Carole pulled out two quite different-looking wedding gowns.

“*I think these are too bohemian,*” Wendy whispered to Frannie. “*What do you think?*”

“I firmly believe that the wedding gown you buy will be the most important purchase you ever make. I chose too quickly, and now look at me, married to Shawn Gabrilska. He is a sex fiend.”

Frannie chose one of the two wedding gowns.

“This is the closest so far. Can I pencil in the changes I would like?”

Frannie penciled in a patchwork pattern down to the sleeves and made the gown longer.

“Can you make this?” Frannie asked.

“The lady in West Allis can, but it takes a few weeks. Do you have that much time?”

“Well, the wedding is on March 20.”

“Ok, I’ll ask the lady in West Allis to expedite this and ship it to me as fast as possible.”

“What if I don’t like it?”

“Well then, don’t buy it,” Wendy said.

"Buy the closest to your taste. It has to be something you feel very good in," Carole added.

They looked through the racks two more times.

"Do you want to drive to West Allis and make your choice there?"

"No, I'll trust the lady. Just send her a Xerox of my sketch."

Carole made a photocopy and gave the sketch back to Frannie.

"Remember, don't show it to your fiancé," Carole said. "It's bad luck."

"Would you like a deposit?" Frannie asked.

"Well, yes, a down payment would be very comforting to me."

"And the lady in West Allis," Wendy added.

"It's only a small shop, you know."

Frannie studied the sketch.

"If that's what you want, Frannie," Wendy said.

"My heart tells me it is so."

"What about Jesus?" Carole said.

"He approves," Frannie said.

"You're sure? Because there's no refund."

"That's okay." Frannie said, "Sooner or later, I'll wear it."

Wendy took her by the arm and pulled her away from the counter.

"Are you really sure about this?"

"I've never been more sure of anything," Frannie said.

They walked out into the bright light of Third Street. When they came to La Cantina, they stopped.

"Let's go in and have a beer or something. This has to be thought through with absolute clarity."

Wendy went in. Frannie followed. They sat at a table. There was a piñata hanging from the ceiling. That was odd because no one had a birthday and there were no children around. Some men on the other side of the restaurant wore Mexican clothes, black with shining bits of silver. The waitress came up. She seemed to find it odd that two women were at the table.

"Would you like a margarita?" She asked.

"Do you have a strawberry margarita?" Wendy said.

"Yes, we can do that for you. What about for you, ma'am?"

“A strawberry margarita would be just lovely,” Frannie said.

The lady came back with two margaritas.

“What would you like for the main course?” the waitress asked. She brushed her black hair back and waited patiently.

“Enchilada verde,” Wendy said.

“I’ll have the same,” Frannie said. “But could I also have another margarita?”

“Of course. And you, senorita?”

Wendy shook her head. “I’m still working on this one.”

The waitress happened to notice the small stack of wedding catalogs.

“Are you two getting married?”

Frannie laughed. “No, not at all. We were in Carole’s choosing a dress. They’re going to make it in West Allis and ship it here. It makes me nervous.”

“It will be alright,” the waitress said.

She walked back to the counter. Mexican music began to play. The waitress served two small wooden bowls of La Cantina’s special salad.

A policeman walked in, smiling at the two women. He pointed to the salads.

“That there is the best salad dressing in Wausau. We bought a bottle of it and took it to the lab to analyze. They got close, but when I gave the recipe to the cook, he shook his head, so I don’t know what’s in there, but it’s very good. What brings you two to La Cantina?”

Frannie cheerfully picked up the stack of wedding catalogs.

“We’re planning my wedding.”

“I’m sorry to hear that, Madame. What about you?” he said to Wendy.

“I’m here to advise her.”

“Have you met the groom?”

“I met him briefly at Christmas but I don’t remember too much. He wasn’t feeling well.”

“Well, maybe you should invite him over and have a second look.”

“Could do, could do.”

"It's what I would do," the cop said as he walked across the dance floor and sat by the two Mexicans. He put a friendly hand on one of the Mexicans' shoulder and began talking Spanish rapidly.

"Where is Cal?" Wendy asked.

"Well, he's in the men's shelter around the corner."

"Frannie, I strongly suggest you invite Cal from the men's shelter to join us right now."

"He'll think I frequent bars."

"Well, so do I," Wendy said.

Frannie raised a forefinger to the waitress and gently jabbed it at her empty margarita glass. The waitress nodded and went back into the kitchen.

"Don't drink too much," Wendy advised.

"Won't you please have another margarita?"

Wendy pointed at her own margarita. The waitress nodded and came back with a margarita. She looked at Frannie carefully.

"You shouldn't drink if you're planning a wedding."

"I won't drink any more."

"I'll make sure of that," Wendy said.

Wendy signaled to the waitress.

"*Teléfono, por favor.*"

"*Si, senorita.*"

The waitress went back one more time. This time she brought a phone with a long cord to Frannie, who dialed the men's shelter. She heard a few clicks. Cal came on the line.

"Hello, darling… I just paid a deposit for my wedding dress at Carole's on Third Street. She's already ordered it from a gown maker in West Allis. It should be here in about a week. It's plaid, white with light beige, and long sleeves… I will feel so good in it… Yes, I will pray to Jesus that it's the right one. Cal darling, listen carefully. I'm in La Cantina on Third Street. I'm with my friend Wendy Gabrilska. She helped me choose the wedding gown, and now she wants to see you. How do you feel about that? You'd just have to walk around the corner onto Third Street. You'll see us there… Okay, dress well, but remember she can be critical."

She hung up and nodded to the waitress, who headed back and took the phone.

"I'm not upmarket. I went to the same school you did."

"No, you went to the Catholic school, and only then you switched to Horace Mann Junior High School. We switched to Wausau Senior High, where you and I became fast friends."

"Yes, you're my best friend," Wendy said. "You rescued me when Bobby Telmer had my hand pinned behind my back at the fence on the far end of the playground. He was busy humping me. I saw you at the other end of the playground and I yelled for you. You came running with a baseball bat with which you hit him on his good leg."

"I did," grinned Frannie. "He was a shit."

"He had polio, you know. Telmer backed off. You really saved me."

"Well I didn't know you at the time but you looked like you needed help and I didn't like Telmer. I knew what kind of a guy he was."

Cal walked into La Cantina. He wore Ralph's clothes, a deep maroon shirt and bright blue trousers with black shoes that sparkled.

He went straight over to Wendy and shook her hand.

"I'm Cal Bedrick."

"I know. I met you at the Jesus house but you weren't feeling well."

After shaking hands with Wendy, Cal came over to Frannie. He bent down and tried to kiss her, but she turned away.

"We're not married yet."

"You're right. Not until March 20."

A strawberry margarita was served to Cal. They all clinked glasses, especially Frannie's, who drank through a straw, as did Cal. Cal put his margarita glass down.

Just then, a guy with heavy motorcycle boots walked in the door. He had longish brown hair. He wore a blue denim jacket and clopped over to Cal.

"Hi Cal," he said.

"Hi Vernon."

"You're here with two ladies. That's not legal, is it?"

They all laughed.

"This is Frannie, who I will marry in less than a month."

"Greetings, Frannie."

"And this is Wendy, Frannie's best friend. She's here to check me out."

Vernon patted Cal on the back. "This is a fine lad, Wendy. I can vouch for him."

Vernon and Cal put their hands on each other's shoulders and sang as they bounced to a rhythm.

We shall be free
We shall be free
We shall be free
When the good Lord sets us free.

Frannie laughed and clapped. "I know that song," she said, "we sing it in church."

"Excuse me," Vernon said, "I'm going to say hello to some of my other friends."

Vernon was shaking hands and lightly punching guys across the floor. He went to the counter and ordered a salad and two beers. There was a Confederate flag stitched to the back of his denim jacket. Wendy stared at it. Cal sat down.

"Frannie, can we leave?" Wendy asked.

"Why?"

"I'm getting just a bit nervous."

"Why?"

"Because of that guy with the Confederate flag on his jacket."

"That's Vernon. He's a good buddy. Oh, here he comes now."

Vernon came back to the table and took Wendy's hands. He hauled her to her feet.

"Frannie, help!"

"Salsa. I asked Hilda to play it slowly," Vernon said.

The music started. It was medium pace. A lot of fellows, many of whom were Mexican, got up and began twirling their partners around in the middle of the floor.

"When I say twirl Wendy, you twirl. Otherwise, do what the women do."

They danced.

"Twirl!"

Wendy twirled but fell on her rump.

"Oh my God," she said.

Vernon hauled her up and took her gently to her seat. She sat slowly.

"Are you alright, Wendy?" Frannie asked.

"I ain't gonna dance that no more," Wendy said.

"Thanks Vernon, but I think I'll sit the next one out," Frannie said.

"Oh, look, it's Pedro's Coffee!"

Cal looked at the menu. "It's awfully strong, Frannie darling."

"I don't give a damn. Order me one."

"They're very expensive, Frannie."

"Don't worry Cal, I'll get it."

Cal raised his hand. Hilda came over.

"A Pedro's Coffee *Especial por mi amiga.*"

Hilda walked away.

"Whoopee!" Frannie said and banged both fists lightly on the table. "Now I'm living!"

"I don't like to see you like this, Frannie," Cal said.

"Well, take a good look."

The lights went out. Everybody oohed and aahed. Frannie kissed Cal on the lips. Some people applauded. Pedro, a short, dark, Mexican man with a short haircut and a Mexican folklore blouse rolled an aluminum cart from the kitchen. Bells jangled in front. Frannie raised a hand.

"*Aquí, señor Pedro,*" she said.

Pedro raised his eyebrows and gave a questioning nod to Cal, who nodded in resignation.

Pedro took a coffee pot with a very long wooden handle. He lighted it with a cigarette lighter and it flamed. There were more oohs and aahs from across the dance floor. Pedro poured in some tequila and some other unknown alcoholic liquid. He poured them all and gave the mixture to Frannie. She slurped. Cal put a hand on her hand to slow her down.

"You are not to dictate to me, Cal, what I may or may not drink. Is that clear?"

Cal leaned back into his chair.

"*Gracias, señor Pedro,*" he said.

Pedro jingled his way back to the kitchen. The lights went on. There was a final burst of applause.

"See, they don't mind," Frannie said.

Frannie drank slowly.

"Jesus! That's strong!"

"Watch your language," Wendy said.

She took another sip and raised her eyebrow.

"*Es muy buena,*" Frannie said to the others sitting across the room. There was some gentle laughter.

The cop left after bumping knuckles with the men at his table. He shook a warning forefinger at Frannie who poured herself the last remnant of Pedro's Special Coffee.

A short while later, the front door opened. Two uniformed cops came in. It got very quiet.

The cops looked around at Vernon and the other guys. Some of the guys hid behind menus.

"Would the idiot who parked behind our patrol car please move it now?" the lead cop said.

"Would the idiot cop who parked right in front of my motorcycle please move it now?" Vernon said.

The Mexicans laughed.

Cal walked to the counter and requested they play "La Bamba" by Richie Valens.

Vernon walked toward the door. As he got to the door, he dropped down suddenly on one knee and spread his arms facing the customers. "Wait! They're playing 'La Bamba.' You can't manhandle me while they're playing Richie Valens singing 'La Bamba.'"

He appealed to the Mexican customers. Many of whom stood up when Vernon raised his hands to the singing of "*Arriba, Arriba!*".

Everybody was dancing, including Cal.

"I've had enough of this," Wendy said. She got up and walked out the door.

Frannie ordered a second Pedro's Special Coffee. The waitress tried to talk her out of it but Frannie shook her head and demanded it. After a while Pedro pushed the jangling coffee cart to Frannie, who was teetering and laughing.

When "La Bamba" was over the cops dragged Vernon out by the armpits while Vernon applauded. The cops pointed to the motorcycle.

"Move your stupid bike back."

"Move your stupid patrol car forward. I was here first."

"Would you like to go to jail?"

"No, been there. Didn't like it."

"Then move your damn bike, Johnny Reb."

Vernon got on his motorcycle and revved it up. It went forward. Everybody in La Cantina heard the metallic scrape against the patrol car. His motorcycle sped off west toward the contiguous township of Schofield.

The cops came back into La Cantina. Frannie was asleep on Cal's right shoulder. She woke up.

"Are we being arrested?" she said.

"Would you like to be?" the cop said.

Frannie shook her head. "Not at all, sir."

"Was that guy a friend of yours?" the cops asked Cal.

"He was an acquaintance, no more."

"Was he a Hells Angel?"

"I don't know. He might have been."

"What was he selling in La Cantina?"

"Whatever it was, we weren't buying."

Frannie leaned again on Cal's shoulder and laughed. "Whoopee!"

It was golden sunset outside across the lawn and sound stage.

"You better take your girlfriend home," one of the cops said.

"As soon as she sobers up," the other cop added.

Frannie threw up just a bit.

"It was just a spit up," she said to Cal. "Don't worry."

"Take her to the bus bench outside."

Cal stood up and motioned to Hilda the sign of writing a check. She came out right away. Frannie's forehead bumped against the tabletop. She snored. Cal paid with Frannie's dollars and then lifted her up.

"Excuse us," Cal said, walked up past the cops out the door, and sat Frannie down on the bus bench and sat down next to her.

"You sound like you're about to throw up big time."

"What do you care?"

"I'm not going to sit next to you."

Cal sidled to the other end of the bus bench. Frannie threw up a second time. She removed her shoes and wiped them on the lawn. She sat down suddenly and slowly put her shoes back on.

"Frannie, you're breaking my heart."

"Oh shut up."

After a while, the two cops came out of La Cantina with a Mexican in handcuffs. One of the cops was carrying a paper bag full of drug capsules. They got into the patrol car and drove the fellow to the police station.

A full moon showed itself on the east side of the grass but below the top timber of the sound stage.

"Frannie, what happened to Wausau?"

"The damn belt line," she slurred. "We still have good new shops on the west side of the lawn, and in summer, we have rock concerts. Very popular."

Cal gently raised her to her feet.

"Can you walk home with me?" Frannie said.

"I will do that, Frannie," he said, "for you."

He followed slowly but she was jogging already, running around the corner of the Wausau Hotel. He jogged to catch up. He turned the corner.

"Oh no!"

Frannie had fallen and was now crawling on hands and knees trying to cross the Stone Street Bridge. Cal ran forward and lifted her from the back to the sidewalk that ran along the stone balustrade. She giggled.

"What's so funny, Frannie?"

"You're holding me by my boobs."

"Well, do you mind?"

"Not really, but I don't want to fall again."

"Put one hand on the banister and your right arm around my waist. I will put my left arm around your waist. When I say left, we will slowly move our left feet forward. When I say right, we put our right feet forward. You keep holding on to the banister as we move along. Together we'll walk home. Is that clear?"

"Clear as ding dong."

They walked very slowly, inching their way over the black Wisconsin River. They got to First Avenue. Cal held up his hand. A car with blazing headlights stopped on First Avenue. Cal eased Frannie across the road onto Stuart Avenue and maneuvered her onto the Sienkiewicz sidewalk past the white propane tanks.

"Oh, it's so nice to be in the kitchen," Frannie said.

"Not yet, Frannie. Those are the propane tanks."

"Well, forgive me for living."

Cal opened the kitchen door. The kitchen lights were on. Cal sat Frannie in the white kitchen chair opposite Joey and the oil portrait of Jesus.

"What the hell have you done to my sister this time?" Joey said.

"She did it to herself," Cal said. "I had nothing to do with it."

Little Brother stood and went to the kitchen drawer, took out two towels and lay them both under Frannie's mouth. He patted her softly on the back.

"That's what you get for forsaking me," he whispered in Frannie's ear.

Cal continuously adjusted the towels. Frannie moved to keep in line with them but did not throw up. Joey came around to Frannie's chair and gently stroked her hair. He stood her up and took her by the arm up the carpeted blue and yellow stairs to her room, where she lay her down in her street clothes. He lay the two towels on her bosom, and also her abdomen. She snored intermittently.

"I don't like you carousing with that son of a bitch," Joey said.

Frannie was asleep but she gave Joey her Sienkiewicz smile.

"I'm going to marry that son of a bitch."

Downstairs, Cal slapped the table. "A ring, we need a ring," he said. "Where the hell can we get rings at this hour?"

"Momma's wedding ring, in their room," Little Brother said.

They all stampeded into the poker room and rummaged through their mother's jewelry box.

"Here it is," Little Brother shouted. He held it up for everyone to see and then put it in his pocket. "I should be the ring bearer."

Chapter 25

A Hmong toddler chased a red-breasted robin, laughing and giggling. His mother picked him up and carried him back down Third Avenue to where the Hmong were settled in the Hollow.

Hmong mothers were allowed to attend kindergarten at Irvin Elementary to be with their youngsters. This caused jealousy among the other mothers. The Hmong had no written language, so they needed extra help from social workers. City taxes had to be raised. Our Lady of the Holy Sepulcher and several Lutheran churches donated boxes of used winter clothing. Some Hmong tried ice skating. Mr. Sippl reopened his store and gave the Hmong cut-rate prices, which angered the other shoppers. Joey led Hmong mothers around the Piggly Wiggly and helped them count their cash at the checkout. Joey did not like them, but Little Brother did not mind. Contrary to expectations, the Hmong did not open Chinese-style laundries.

One enterprising Hmong opened a fish store next to the Hebrew Graveyard on Grand Avenue. Nobody understood how he got sea fish since Wausau was miles away from any ocean.

He began to ponder the strange six-pointed stars on the tombstone to his right. He could not figure them out. He asked his social worker. She could not figure them out. One evening he took a walk around the west side of town. He heard a strange chanting from a stone building with the same six-pointed star on the door. He put his ear to the door and listened carefully. He carefully opened the heavy wooden door. He went in. A guard with a revolver stopped him.

"You're not Jewish."

The Hmong backed away, grinned, and bowed.

He backed out the door and went back to his home behind the fish store. The next day he asked his social worker if there was a company that could print out business cards. He drew a picture of a six-pointed star and a fish with the address in a rectangle around it to show it was a card. He mimed bowing, introducing himself with a handshake to the social worker, and handing her the card. She took him to Emmons Stationery downtown, where they printed fifty cards. The next night he went back to the stone building with the strange six-pointed star and tried to push it open, but it was locked. He went back home. Every night for a week he went back to that building with his business card, and eventually, on a Friday, the door opened. He went in. The guard was alert but did not draw his pistol.

"You again?"

He pointed to a bench against the far wall. "Sit."

The Hmong smiled. The guard mimicked sitting. The Hmong sat on the bench and smiled, fingering his fifty business cards. After a while, the service was over. Jews came out with the rabbi. Rabbi Matzner had been a German butcher. He escaped through meadows where the bodies had all been blown open. He applied to be a rabbi when Wausau Synagogue advertised the position, and he got the job. His wife was a severe-looking woman with black hair pulled straight back into a bun. They had one son, Gary, who was frail and played the violin quite well. Several years later, Gary was killed in a traffic accident on Brooklyn Bridge.

As the male Jews left, they put their skullcaps either into a cardboard box or into their coat pockets, nodded to the rabbi, and said goodnight in Hebrew: "Laila Tov." The rabbi responded, "Laila Tov." Some women hugged the rabbi, and some said "Laila Tov" as they walked down the sidewalk. The Hmong handed each of the Jews a business card. The lobby now had only the rabbi, the guard, and the Hmong, who stood and smiled.

"Okay," Rabbi Matzner said, "what is this all about?"

"I don't know," the guard said. "He doesn't speak English. He seems to be a businessman selling fish."

The Hmong handed the rabbi a business card, smiling, and passed the guard a business card too. There was no name on the business card.

"Maybe he's Chinese," the guard said.

"No, the Chinese would have a name on it. The Hmong have no alphabet." The rabbi turned to the Hmong and asked, "Hmong?"

The Hmong nodded vigorously. He and the rabbi and the guard shook hands. The Hmong figured it was time to leave, so he backed out the door reciting the two English words he now knew.

"Laila Tov."

Other Hmong were hired by the city to clear sidewalks, sweep roads, and other maintenance jobs. They also received checks from the city. This angered many of the whites because city taxes went up. Gangs formed among the whites, and then gangs formed among the Hmong. Finally, a white guy took his rifle and shot dead a Hmong.

Chapter 26

It was intensely dark on March 19, the day of the worst ice storm in Wausau's history. Duck Island was sheeted over, both bare branches and new reeds on the shore. The lodge was also sheeted in ice. Hail banged against the men's shelter windows. There was a yellow-green light in Cal's bedroom in the men's shelter.

Three-quarter-life-size transparent dolls in vivid Chinese colors moved around the bed, watching him. Their faces were white with slits revealing black eyes. Two other dolls watched from the foot of the bed, saying nothing but watching intently. One was wearing a mask that made it look like Che Guevara. The other had a blank white face.

A terracotta pot with red geraniums came slowly down from the ceiling.

A well-dressed girl of about 22, taking big steps, went around Cal's bed guiding the others. She wore black-and-white diamond patterns and black trousers and slippers that were curled up at the front.

An old lady in a rocking chair was knitting while keeping vigil. A collie dog was resting at her feet, also keeping vigil. A black and white diamond pattern decorated the floor.

Cal sat up, bewildered.

"Ralph, wake up. I see strange things, and they're very, very real."

"Don't call Mr. Dula. If you do, he'll put you in the mental ward. You don't want that."

Cal put both hands to his face. "It must be because of the wedding. Oh God, Ralph, what have I done?"

"You've done the best thing ever. You're marrying a beautiful girl who will take care of you and your family."

There was a long silence. The hail battered the shelter building.

"Lord a-mercy," Ralph said.

After a while, Cal fell asleep.

* * *

There was a mouth at his ear.

"Wake up, Cal my boy."

"Huh . . . who are you?"

"I am your lord and master . . ." said Mr. Dula. "Wake up . . . today is the day."

"For what?"

"You're getting married today, just before noon."

"Oh God."

Ralph came into the room holding a tuxedo in his hands.

"Undress, my boy. It's not black because it's a funeral, its black because you're ending this part of your life."

Ralph pulled Cal up by the hand. Cal stepped groggily off the mattress onto the floor. Ralph quickly put on the tuxedo top and tuxedo trousers, buttoned the trousers.

"Mr. Dula, is this turkey ready to waddle?"

"Yes, he's the bee's knees. Cal, I will escort you over the bridge to Frannie because this town is iced over."

They put on overcoats and galoshes and went out.

It was much lighter, with a few sprinkles of ice. They walked onto the bridge. Mr. Dula had his elbow crooked around Cal's right hand. Cal's other hand was on the concrete banister.

They slowly followed a fellow who was sprinkling sand and salt from a cart onto the walkway. The Wisconsin River was silver with streaks of dark blue. The flat roof of the Junior Game Warden Lodge was covered with ice, and the porch and steps were completely iced over. There were little footprints of white snow all around.

They crossed First Avenue, stepping carefully. Mr. Dula knocked on the Sienkiewicz pantry door. Frannie was in her slip.

 She shrieked and ran upstairs. Little Brother opened the door.

"Just in time for eggs on toast and coffee, guys," he said.

They went in, took off their coats, and warmed up. Joey made coffee.

They stopped eating when they saw Frannie come down the steps in her wedding dress. Slowly and shyly, holding onto the banister.

They stood.

Joey put his hands over Cal's eyes. "You're not supposed to see this."

Her top was white with beige patches. Her skirt was white and with beige ruffles. Her shoes were patched to match the top. Her sleeves were long, down to the wrists, and her neck was fully covered by small beige and white ruffles.

Her freshly washed hair was heavily curled. She looked around shyly.

"Do I look okay?"

"You're beautiful!" Cal said.

She turned around to show them her back and then sat down and drank coffee. She did not eat for fear of throwing up later.

She slapped the table.

"Who called for a taxi?" she asked.

Nobody answered.

"It's my wedding day. Do I have to do everything?"

She was on the phone for a long time.

"Forty-five minutes? That's too long. I'm getting married today… Right now! I know you have a lot of customers in weather like this, but they can't all be getting married, can they? We're at 38 Stuart Avenue. Please, please hurry." Frannie hung up angrily.

"We will form a cortege from the church to Bill's Fine Foods after the wedding. We'll have our wedding dinner there with our best friends and loved ones." She turned to Jesus. "Please make it stop raining or hailing, and warm it up a bit."

"Let me see the rings, Little Brother," Joey said.

Little Brother opened a blue velvet jeweler's box carefully. The ring was opal surrounded by diamonds.

"It's, beautiful," Frannie said. "What about Cal's ring?"

"I don't have one," Cal said.

Mr. Dula turned. "Take this, my boy, and for God's sake don't lose it." He gave Cal his own thick gold wedding ring. Cal gave the ring to Little Brother who put it carefully in the blue velvet ring box and placed the box on the kitchen table.

"Do you know what to do with it?" Joey asked.

"I put them on the altar, and Father Leszinski will sprinkle holy water on them and bless them."

"Taxi is here!" Frannie yelled.

They all ran out. Frannie held her skirt up not to get muddied. Now the hail had turned to rain and was coming down very hard. Joey held an umbrella over Frannie.

"Oh damn, oh damn, oh damn it."

Joey locked the door. It thundered.

Frannie and Cal got in the back seat. Joey, Mr. Dula, and Little Brother squeezed beside the driver in the front seat.

"Hell of a day to get married," the driver said. "Where are we going?"

"Our Lady of the Holy Sepulcher," said Joey. "You can drive on the lawn, sir. I will tip you handsomely."

He made a slow U-turn on sanded gravel. The taxi moved slowly, slipping slightly on the mud to Fourth Avenue.

"Where are the rings?" Cal said.

"WE FORGOT THE RINGS!" Frannie screamed.

"Turn around!" Joey shouted to the driver. "Back to the house!"

The driver made another very slow U-turn and skidded to a stop in front of the Sienkiewicz house. Little Brother burst out the door and ran into the kitchen with all the speed the Lord granted him. The ring box was still on the kitchen table where Little Brother had left it. Little Brother ran out without locking the door and jumped back into the front seat, all wet, his hair plastered.

"Let me see the rings, Little Brother," Frannie said.

Little Brother carefully opened the box. The rings were still there.

"Thank you Jesus," she said.

"Thank you Jesus," Little Brother said.

"Thank you Jesus," Cal said.

"Thank you Jesus," Mr. Dula said.

"Thank you Jesus," Joey said.

"Thank you Jesus," the driver said.

The driver turned onto Fourth past the synagogue, but the road was blocked. A tow truck was at right angles to the street, inching up to two cars that had crumpled together. A third car was lodged against a light pole. Amber lights were flashing before and after the wreck. A policeman came to the driver's door.

"No going further. There's a wreck up ahead."

"But we're getting married!" Frannie yelled.

"Right now!" Cal yelled.

"You can get married right in the taxi. Stranger things have happened in taxis."

"Everybody out," Mr. Dula said. "I'll pay the driver."

"Frannie and Cal, I've got an umbrella, and I want Frannie to use it. Her hair must not get wet," Joey said.

"We'll walk the rest of the way. It's not that far."

Everybody got out and began walking.

"My shoes! My shoes!" Frannie shouted.

Mr. Dula and Joey carefully lifted Frannie by the crooks of her elbows about two inches off the road. Cal reached down and picked up her shoes. They all trundled to the open door of Our Lady of the Holy Sepulcher.

It was getting unseasonably warm. The sun was out through the clouds.

Orange nasturtiums grew thick along the base of the church, as did red and white geraniums. A train went roaring by on the trestle bridge. Frannie and her friends stood to the right of the dark doorway of the church. Frannie's red hair, which now looked red and gold, had been curled courtesy of an expensive hairdresser, Vivian's, downtown. She looked resplendent: her sparkling green eyes were brighter than normal, and so was the gold cross around her neck. She wore an immaculate white linen jacket over her blouse. A cluster of her special and longtime friends, Wendy Gabrilska, Gina Durkee, Marsha

Brandenburg, Margie Linke, and Hildegard Tomek, clustered around her, patting her, smoothing her cheeks, laughing nervously, and kissing her.

"I want to get this over with," Frannie said.

A ruby-throated hummingbird buzzed outside the rosette window. A red-winged blackbird nested on the roof of the church.

Cal, Joey, and Little Brother stood to the left of the open dark doorway with Ralph and Mr. Dula. Cal's eyes were twitching from nervousness. Cal's black tuxedo was neatly creased. He wore black trousers and black shoes. His socks were somewhat red and green. His white boutonniere had somewhat collapsed. His eyes were black and large. His hair was carefully combed. He nervously paced the doorway. To his left were Joey and Little Brother, wearing deep blue dress coats with shiny lapels and bowties where the ties tilted downwards at a 45-degree angle. Ralph was in a maroon jacket with deep red buttons and deep blue creased slacks. Mr. Dula, who wore bright yellow shirt and green trousers, talked gently to Cal to calm him down. His hair had been curled. He kept one arm on Cal's shoulder as though for friendship, or to keep Cal from running away.

After a while, Father Leszinski, wearing all white, came to the door and said gently, "Witnesses please."

Mr. Dula and Wendy Gabrilska went into the church. Father Leszinski showed them where to stand and came back to the doorway.

"And now, please, friends and family may enter. Friends and family of the bride to the left, friends and family of the groom to the right."

The fairly large congregation found their seats amongst the pews.

Cal realized the priest was waiting for him.

"Cal, are you ready?" Father Leszinski said softly.

"As ready as I'll ever be."

"Larry, you are the ring bearer. Do you have the rings?"

Little Brother pulled out the blue velvet jewelry box from his coat pocket.

"Now, you won't drop it?"

Little Brother closed the box and put it back in his pocket. "Absolutely not."

"You would be surprised what happened with a nervous groom. I've seen it all. Please, follow me to the front of the aisle."

With Little Brother to his right and Cal to his left, Father Leszinski walked meditatively. The sun was exceedingly bright in the rosette window and beamed red and blue patches onto the church floor. The interior of the church was filled with red gladioli.

"Those flowers must have cost a fortune," Cal said.

"Don't worry about it," Little Brother said.

The priest turned to face the congregation. He gestured for Little Brother to sit in the leftmost part of the first pew. Little Brother sat.

"Cal, you move closer to Little Brother, but stay standing."

"Why isn't anything happening?" Cal asked.

"It is customary to wait for the bride."

The congregation had all kinds of hair colors: black, brown, red, Scandinavian white, and they all wore their very best Sunday clothes. Sister Elizabeth played two hymns, and the congregation sang standing.

Joey brought in Frannie with elbows tenderly hooked, her red hair shining and green eyes ablaze with glory. She could not stop smiling.

"You may give the bride away," the priest said to Joey once the hymns ended.

Joey looked suddenly terribly forlorn and frightened. He let go of Frannie. The priest gestured to the seat beside Little Brother. Joey sat next to Little Brother.

Frannie was very nervous but kept smiling as she looked forward toward the priest and the altar. Cal surreptitiously turned to look at the rear gothic window. A ruby-throated hummingbird poked at the window. It was probably the same as the one that had been outside, for how many ruby-throated hummingbirds can be attracted to a Catholic church? It was very quiet. Cal kept looking at the rear window. "How serene," he said.

Suddenly, two monarch butterflies flew in and mated on the back of a pew. There was a small desk in the dark hallway to the vestry with a heavy church registry on top. Wendy and Mr. Dula sat on each side. There was a small horizontal fluorescent light in a brass tubular case overhead. Mr. Dula stood and pulled the golden chain, and the light gleamed over the open registry. When the time came, Cal and Frannie would sign the registry, it would be witnessed, and that would be that.

Father Leszinski spread his arms in a welcoming gesture to the congregation.

"You may sit. … In the Name of the Father, the Son, and the Holy Spirit, I welcome you friends and neighbors, Catholic or otherwise, to Our Lady of the Holy Sepulcher. Please be seated for the liturgy."

Chairs were brought out for Cal and Frannie.

"Mr. Dula, you are the witness for Cal Bedrick. Will you please come and read from Psalms? For those who are not Catholic, let me explain. This will be a nuptial mass. That means that we will do the Holy Sacraments to praise the Lord Jesus and, in the middle thereof, the bride and groom will exchange their holy vows, after which I shall pronounce them man and wife."

Mr. Dula stood and smiled. He stepped out from the witness booth and came up behind the altar where the Holy Bible was open to a page in Psalms.

"'Blessed is everyone who fears the Lord, who walks in his ways,'" Mr. Dula read. "'Your wife will be like a fruitful vine within your house; your children will be like olive shoots around your table. Lo, thus shall the man be blessed who fears the Lord.'"

Cal's eyes brightened. "I know this one," he said.

"Praise be to God," the congregation said.

Mr. Dula put the Bible back on the lectern, walked carefully to the vestry's registration desk, and sat down on a chair by its side.

"Wendy Gabrilska, you will be Frannie's witness. Could you please now come to the lectern and read from the New Testament?"

The priest opened the New Testament to a red velvet marker. Wendy, with tears in her eyes, began reading.

"Love is patient and kind; love is not jealous or boastful; it is not arrogant or rude. Love does not insist on its own way; it is not irritable or resentful; it does not rejoice at wrong but rejoices in the right. Love bears all things, hopes all things, and endures all things. Love is stronger than death."

Frannie carefully wiped a tear away with the back of her hand. Wendy walked carefully and sat on the chair on the other side of the registry.

"Please stand for the gospel acclamation," Father Leszinski said.

Everybody stood. Cal and Frannie stood. The chairs were taken away.

"Dearly beloved," Father Leszinski began, "this Mass will include the wedding and holy vows of Cal Bedrick and Frances Sienkiewicz."

Father Petrus rang a bell. It was the Eucharist. All those who were Catholic stood.

Father Leszinski blessed the red wine. Father Petrus gave some to Frannie, some to Cal, then delicately wiped their lips with a small but pretty towel. Father Petrus put the wine goblet back on the altar. Father Petrus rang the bell again.

Peewee Szabo and Terry Grabow began punching each other in the rear pew until Mrs. Szabo separated them.

Father Leszinski blessed the wafers, which were on a silver platter and resting on the altar. Father Petrus gave a wafer to Frannie, who was kneeling at the altar, and then to Cal, also kneeling at the altar.

Father Petrus sat down against the wall. Father Leszinski spread his arms out to the congregation.

"My dear friends and neighbors, this does not conclude the Mass. We still have to hear the holy vows. I have known the Sienkiewicz family since Frannie was a few days old."

Frannie laughed, and so did her friends.

"Her father, Jack Sienkiewicz, was a devout Catholic and a fine man who valued his job in the Central Wausau Hotel. Frannie's mother, Anna, was the most wonderful of women and equally devout. I did not know Cal Bedrick's father, who was a faithful member of Mount Sinai Synagogue. Cal Bedrick's father was a distinguished professor of chemistry and highly respected at the University of Wisconsin Extension Center. Cal Bedrick was an outstanding scholar at Wausau Senior High School and graduated second in his class. Despite his youth, he has traveled much and experienced much. He and Frannie are perfect complements. I have met with them both and explained the doctrine. They are very much in love with each other. I do not doubt their sincerity. Frannie will bring forth many fine little Catholics."

People chuckled. Frannie blushed.

"You may hold hands, Cal and Frannie."

They held hands, smiling broadly. Cal was breathing hard, and so was Frannie.

"Do you, Calum Bedrick, take this woman, Frances Gail Sienkiewicz, to be your lawful wedded wife, to have and to hold from this day forward, in sickness and health, in richness and poverty, till death do you part?"

Frannie mouthed, *"Say 'I do'."*

"I do," Cal said.

The priest turned to Frannie.

"Frances Gail Sienkiewicz, do you take this man, Calum Bedrick, to be your lawful wedded husband to have and hold from this day forward, in sickness and health, in richness and poverty, till death do you part?"

"I DO," Frannie said.

Father Leszinski nodded to Little Brother. Little Brother pulled out the jewelry box from his coat pocket and handed it to Father Leszinski, who opened it and sprinkled holy water on the rings. He gave a ring to Cal and said, "Cal Bedrick, you may put this on the ring finger of Frances Sienkiewicz while saying 'With this ring I thee wed.'"

Little Brother sat down. Cal slowly slipped the ring down Frannie's left ring finger. It was a beautiful ring. Frannie watched it come towards the tip of her finger.

"With this ring, I thee —"

The congregation gasped because not only had the ring left Cal's hand, it had flown out in an arc towards the vestry hall.

"No, no, no," Frannie said.

Cal stared at Wendy Gabrilska, who had neatly caught the ring in her left hand and brought it forward to Cal.

"B-bless you, Wendy," Frannie said, drying her eyes with the backs of her hands.

"Thank you. You may give the ring to Cal Bedrick and return to your place."

Wendy went back to her place by the registry.

Frannie held out her left hand.

"Cal, you may now put the ring on the ring finger of your beloved and say, 'With this ring I thee wed.'" Cal gently put the ring on her ring finger. "With this ring …" Frannie looked at him closely and said the words, "I thee …" the congregation held its breath, and everybody said together, "wed."

Frannie looked at the ring fondly. The diamonds sparkled.

The priest took Cal's ring out of the box and gave it to Frannie, who looked at it lovingly. Frannie placed the ring on Cal's ring finger and said loudly, "With this ring, I thee wed."

The congregation laughed gently.

"Cal, you may now kiss the bride."

"Really?"

Somebody in the congregation yelled, "Come on Cal." Cal leaned forward. Frannie turned her face so her cheek was there for kissing. Cal put one hand on her neck and then kissed her long and hard.

Father Leszinski held his right hand over Cal, his left hand over Frannie, and said loudly, "I now pronounce you man and wife."

There was instantaneous loud applause. Cal and Frannie held hands. Father Leszinski grinned. He stepped forward and addressed the congregation. "I have seen rings dropped, I have seen grooms and brides forget their lines and forget the names of the person they are marrying, but I have never seen a ring flying through the air quite like that … Let's be grateful to the Holy Spirit that returns to us that which we thought we had lost."

There were chuckles from the congregation. A scarlet tanager flew by the rear gothic window.

"Cal and Frannie will now sign their names in the official church registry for future generations, and they will be witnessed by Wendy Gabrilska and Mr. Dula. Then they will walk out, all things completed. I will shake your hands at the door, and you can follow them to the outside world."

Father Petrus stood up from his chair and conducted them to the open registry book. He handed Cal a black pen and pointed to a place for Cal to sign. Then he did the same for Frannie. Wendy Gabrilska signed as a witness. Mr. Dula signed as a witness.

Suddenly a brown bird with a broken wing flopped down the vestry hall. Wendy Gabrilska carefully picked it up, held it to her breast, and gently opened the side vestry door to let the creature out.

Father Petrus gestured to Father Leszinski.

"I will now lead the husband and wife to the main church door, then everyone may leave," Father Leszinski said.

Cal and Frannie walked slowly and meditatively behind Father Leszinski down the aisle to the open church door. All three stopped and crossed themselves in front of the polychrome Jesus, then they continued down the aisle. The door was open.

Father Leszinski stopped at the door. Beyond him was a bright green new lawn. Father Leszinski hugged Frannie and shook Cal's hand.

"May you be with Jesus, always. Cal, you are always welcome in this church. You have married a very fine girl. She will take good care of you."

"I know."

Cal and Frannie went out onto the lawn.

Joey followed. He gave an envelope to Father Leszinski.

"For the church."

"Thank you for your generous contribution to the church, Joey," Father Leszinski said.

Father Petrus spread his arms and moved them forward, signifying that everybody should leave.

Everybody went out and stood on the church lawn in the bright sunshine.

Women hugged and kissed Frannie. The first was her best friend, Wendy.

"*You just made the worst mistake of your life*," Wendy whispered.

"Shush Wendy, it's my wedding."

"Oh, the ring! How much did it cost?"

"Don't be nosey."

All the other women gathered around Frannie to ogle the ring, which she flashed happily in front of their faces.

On the other side of the dark church door Mr. Dula hugged Cal. "This marriage had better work because we've had an influx of disturbed veterans who ended up on the street and have all ended up in the shelter. There's no bed for you."

"I now have a very nice bed, thank you," Cal said.

Ralph straightened out the boutonniere on Cal's lapel.

"You did very well Cal, for your first time."

"I had no idea where I was," Cal confessed.

Chapter 27

The wedding couple walked hand in hand down Fourth Avenue, followed by Joey, Little Brother, and Charles, who began to sing a Polish military song. A cortege of Frannie's young lady friends, with Wendy Gabrilska in the lead, crossed down to Third Avenue and continued south to Bill's Fine Foods on the right. A slender pipe with holes sent water spraying into a pool of rainbow trout. There was a glass bubble machine dispensing pellets of trout food. Wendy put in a quarter, turned the knob, and let everybody take a pellet or two from her hand. The trout must have been ravenous because they broke the turquoise water to snap at the pellets still in the air.

The owner of Bill's Fine Foods, Mr. Bill Hoeft, opened the door with a broad smile.

"Hello Frannie, you look so beautiful," he said. He turned to Cal. "You must be the lucky fellow."

"I am."

"Please come in. I reserved the entire restaurant for the wedding feast. I do get to kiss the bride, don't I?"

Bill kissed Frannie and led the bridal couple to chairs at the end of a long dining table. Wendy and Little Brother sat respectively on the left and right. Joey and Charles took up chairs at the very far end of the dining table.

They went in. There were bouquets in glass vases on a long table covered in white linen. On the wall, Mr. Hoeft had put a sign: "Congratulations Frannie and Cal".

Mr. Hoeft's daughter Cathy brought in excellent bread and creamy Wisconsin butter. She wore glasses that were pointed at the ends. She was short and had curly hair. She grinned.

"Cal, Cal, it's you getting married."

"You better believe it."

"Oh Frannie, did you know what you were doing?" Cathy laughed.

"Yes, he's a fine young man, and I love him," Frannie said.

"Well, he was in my English class, and he sure knew a lot."

Charles smuggled an excellent seven-year-old bottle of Canadian whiskey to Joey.

"Cathy, can you please bring us shot glasses so we can make a toast to the bride and groom," Joey said.

"You're not supposed to bring your own liquor in here," Cathy said.

"Oh come on Cathy, how often do we get married?" Charles said.

"I'll go ask my father."

Cathy went into the kitchen and returned with a tray full of shot glasses. She gave one to each. Joey poured whiskey into everybody's glass.

"Hey, what about me," Cathy said.

Joey poured her some whiskey too.

Joey stood up and raised his glass. "All rise." Everybody stood. "Welcome to you all, and thank you for coming to the wedding banquet for the most beautiful sister in the world and the dope she married. No, I didn't mean that, Cal. You're not a dope. You have a lot of potential; I know because you have never used it. It's still there."

People chuckled. Joey wiped his eyes. "I conclude my toast by wishing them the happiest possible marriage, which they both richly deserve, and as many children as they can handle, all Catholic, of course. To Cal Bedrick and Frannie Bedrick."

"To Cal Bedrick and Frannie Bedrick," everybody repeated and drank. The whiskey was strong, and Frannie coughed a little bit after drinking.

"Don't let Cal drink too much, or he won't be able to perform," Marsha said.

Everybody laughed.

"Charles, please fill the glasses but not for Cal," Joey said. Charles filled everybody's glasses but not Cal's. He patted Cal's head and said, "Good luck, soldier."

"It's your turn to toast, Cal," Joey said.

Cal raised his nearly empty glass. "Yes, I am equally happy to see all of you here to help celebrate the wedding of the most beautiful girl I have ever seen and probably the smartest. As some of you know, I had a bit of a rough patch before coming back to Wausau. In other words, I didn't know who I was or where I was or why I was. I was living in the men's shelter and after a long while being hired by the grace of God and the generosity of Joey Sienkiewicz. I was having breakfast with the Sienkiewicz family. Gradually I realized I could not live without Frannie, so I proposed. It was on Valentine's Day. When she said yes, it felt, and I am speaking sincerely now, that God himself had said yes to me. So now we can all raise our glasses to good health and joy for the bride and groom, and the Sienkiewicz family."

Everybody raised their glass and drank. Cal kissed Frannie on the lips. They all sat down.

Suddenly Mr. Hoeft and Cathy came through the kitchen door. Each was smiling broadly and bringing a platter of grilled salmon, roast potatoes, baby tomatoes, and asparagus. Everybody oohed and aahed. Cathy brought in beer glasses and bottles of the Polish beer Kozlak. Charles and Joey popped the lids off and drank quickly. Little Brother also drank.

"You should get married more often, Frannie," Little Brother said.

Everybody laughed.

"Don't wait. Eat," Frannie said.

Everybody picked up their forks and began to eat dinner. Forks and knives clinked.

"Delicious," Margie said.

Joey called to Cathy, "Could we have some more beer please Cathy?"

Cathy went back into the kitchen and came out with a tray full of Kozlak beer and said cheerfully, "Who wants more Kozlak?"

Several hands went up. Cathy served.

Wendy Gabrilska was getting sloshed. "What the hell did you see in this guy?" she asked Frannie.

"He can be very charming."

"Oh really? Has he ever done it before?"

"Nope," Cal said.

"Neither have I, so please shush, Wendy."

Wendy patted Cal on the hand. "If you need some instruction, I'll come along."

"No thank you," Cal said.

"Is it really that difficult?" Frannie said.

"Depends on your ambition."

Wendy Gabrilska drank some more whiskey. Her eyes were getting blurred. She held Frannie's hand and whispered, *"Don't let him put it in your mouth."*

"What?"

"Don't let him go into your backside," she whispered.

"Wendy Gabrilska, you're my best friend, but I really have had enough of this."

"What was she talking about?" Cal asked.

"Men will sexually degrade any woman they can at any time," Wendy said.

Everybody drank more whiskey and more Polish beer. Cathy brought another tray of Kozlak and took away the empty plates.

Mr. Hoeft brought in ice cream dishes with chocolate sundaes and a cherry on top. This caused merriment. He passed the desserts around.

"Fran," Wendy said, "Do you have your cherry?"

This caused louder laughter. Frannie blushed.

"I don't get it," Cal said.

"No, but you will tonight," Wendy said.

"Wendy, please, can we elevate the conversation closer to the angels," Frannie said.

"Sorry." Wendy dabbed at her eyes with her napkin. "My own marriage has been such a catastrophe."

"Can't you get a divorce? You're not Catholic," Cal said.

"No, but I'm hooked on him."

"Does he beat you?" Frannie asked.

"Mentally," Wendy said.

Everybody ate their cherries and then spooned into their chocolate sundaes.

"This is just so fabulous," Gina said.

The dessert goblets were taken away.

Bill Hoeft had a terrific collection of Polish and German polkas, which he now played. Joey danced with Wendy. Charles danced with Frannie.

Cal suddenly ran out of the restaurant. He clapped a young man on the back.

"Julius!"

The guy turned. He had curly white hair, rimless glasses, a terrific smile, perfect teeth, gray suede trousers, a gray suede jacket, and expensive gray suede shoes.

"Cal Bedrick, old man! My name is now Joshua Klein, much more Jewish, don't you think? Drove my mother crazy."

"How do you like it in Canada?" Cal said.

"It's a lot better than this stupid country."

"I heard you were married" Cal said.

"Yes, to a Japanese woman."

"Of course."

"She likes hash and mescaline. I like acid and fine Canadian whiskey. If you do anything good for yourself Cal, you'll move to Canada."

"Well, maybe I will. It sounds wonderful."

"What's going on in Bill's?" Joshua asked.

"It's a wedding party."

"Who got married?"

Cal grinned. "I did."

Joshua punched Cal playfully. "No kidding. Who did you talk into it?"

"You'll never guess."

"Chris Carsten, of course."

"Nope."

"I give up. Who?"

"Frannie Bedrick, formerly Sienkiewicz."

Joshua laughed heartily. "You're joking, aren't you? How did you convince her?"

"She fell in love with me. I had nothing to do with it."

"Well, this is terrific. Here's a wedding present," Joshua said.

He reached into the inside of his jacket pocket and pulled out a small cellophane envelope with four large red pills, each divided down the middle.

"Put these in your tuxedo pocket. Here comes trouble," Joshua said.

Wendy marched out of Bill's Fine Foods glaring at Joshua who grinned amicably.

"Go dance with Frannie, take over from Charles. I'll handle this," Wendy said to Cal. She put a hand on Cal's shoulder. He went back inside the restaurant and kissed Frannie on the dance floor. Charles moved away.

Outside, Wendy's voice got shrill. She was obviously telling Joshua that he wasn't wanted at Bill's Fine Foods. Joshua grinned sheepishly and went by the trout pond, looking in through the glass door and the polka dancers. Cathy came to the door, curious. Wendy went up the steps. They both disregarded Joshua who had walked far away.

"*Don't let him in here,*" Wendy whispered to Cathy.

Cathy nodded. They closed the door behind them.

Wendy resumed doing the polka with her dance partner, Joey, who laughed because Wendy was a bit clumsy. Suddenly Mr. Hoeft was doing the polka with Marsha. They were both very good.

Charles lifted the whiskey bottle and drank from it looking at the ceiling.

"That was to you, Frannie. I pray for you and pray that the angels look after you. Don't worry about me."

Wendy took the bottle out of Charles's hands and filled her shot glass. Then she filled Frannie's. Frannie and Wendy clinked glasses and drank them down. At the other end of the table, Charles whispered urgently to Joey. Alarmed, Joey stood up. Wendy walked quickly to his end of the table and stole the bottle of aged whiskey and carried it quickly to the trout end of the table where she sat even more heavily and with two hands filled Frannie's empty shot glass and her own. Frannie and Wendy giggled, clinked glasses, and emptied their whiskey glasses. Joey came from out of nowhere and snatched the whiskey bottle.

"Frannie, no more," Joey said.

"I'll have more if I want more."

"I'm paying for this bottle and I'm saying no, you can't have any more."

Cal tapped Charles on the shoulder. Frannie smiled the Sienkiewicz smile as she and Cal moved in unison through the polka steps.

"Who was that guy, Cal?"

"An old high school buddy."

"Was he selling anything?"

"I wasn't buying, Frannie."

"Wendy seems to think you must have bought something."

"Cross my heart and hope to die if I ever tell a lie, I didn't buy anything from Joshua, Frannie."

It was getting dark outside. The long shadows from the west side of Third Avenue were now reaching up into the buildings on the east side. Cathy came by with a fresh pot of strong coffee. Marsha and Joey pointed to their small coffee cups and looked at Cathy's face. Cathy smiled and poured, then went back to the kitchen. Joey stood up, opened his wallet, and signed a check, which he tore out and took back to the kitchen and gave to Mr. Hoeft.

"You haven't filled in the amount, Joey," Mr. Hoeft said.

"I leave that to you."

"Are you sure you can cover the check I will now write?"

"Try it and we'll see," Joey said as he left the kitchen.

Others were already outside, tossing in food pellets to the trout in the trout pond. A few had crossed Third Avenue. They were walking happily but slowly in the direction of the Sienkiewicz home.

The polka music was still playing. Frannie nuzzled up to Cal who had his arm around her shoulder. The others had caught up to them on the east side of Third Avenue. Several drivers honked when they saw the bridal couple. Little Brother had painted with soap on the windows: "Tonight's the Night", and in the other window, "Just Married".

Frannie and Cal hugged each one of the guests in turn. The threesome of Charles, Joey, and Little Brother half danced down through pink, orange, and purple shadows, singing a long forgotten Polish war song, to Charles's house. Wendy was the last guest to congratulate Frannie.

When Wendy hugged Cal she whispered, *"Take good care of my best friend, Cal, I love her as much as you do. If that white haired guy snuck anything into one of your pockets, throw it away tonight."*

"I promise," Cal said.

She squeezed Frannie hard. "I have to congratulate you Frannie. You look so beautiful in your West Allis wedding gown, and I love your amendments to it."

"I was inspired by you, Wendy."

"My wedding dress was a mistake, yours was glorious. But I'm worried about you, Frannie."

"Don't be. I've got Jesus on my side."

They kissed on the lips. Wendy went in past the soaped windows. The last she saw of Frannie, she and Cal were groping their way through the dark to the stairwell.

The linoleum floor seemed to have curved and blackened. The oil heater had turned deep purple. On the right was the red couch. There was a strange-looking furry animal on the red couch. The animal had sharp claws and a black snout. It turned out to be Little Brother's washed laundry waiting to be ironed.

"Do you iron their clothes?"

"Nope. I may be the girl of the house, but they tend to do what I say."

Cal paused. "Now what."

"Kneel and pray."

They knelt on prayer pillows in front of the home altar. The red and green lights were dancing around the door.

Frannie opened the door to reveal the Virgin Mary, the lamb, and the magi. Frannie moved the three magi left over from

Christmas a few steps closer to the Virgin Mary and made them kneel and bow on their articulated legs. The Virgin Mary still had her eyes inscrutably closed, but gestured generously, her hands resting on her knees, open palmed. Frannie pressed a little button, and stars started turning around the Virgin Mary.

"Hail Mary full of grace ... May I be worthy ... to have a child this night, in your honor, to have and to hold and bring him to Jesus Christ. Amen." Frannie whispered.

Cal prayed silently, *"Hail Mary, Mother of God, full of grace, I pray with all my heart that I can complete my task tonight."*

They both slowly got up. The walls were pink, orange, and purple due to the sun setting through the window. They went up the stairs hand in hand. Their hands were cold. It was nearly black now outside.

"I'm getting frightened," Frannie said.

"Me too."

There was a blue rectangle, pebbled and moist, letting in the twilight. It must have been the bathroom window.

Trembling, Frannie opened the door to her bedroom, which was dark. She turned on the light.

Her brothers had put Easter lilies and red gladioli around the room.

They sat awkwardly next to each other on the edge of the bed, not knowing what to do or say. Their legs swung slowly. Cal put a tentative arm around her shoulder. She stiffened.

"It's too bright. But with the light off, it's too dark," Frannie said.

Cal padded downstairs, turned left over the linoleum of the living room and opened the liquor cabinet. He took out the four brass angels, a white candle, a brass candle holder, and a box of small wooden matches and carried them carefully upstairs. He backed into Frannie's room and set them on her dresser under the photograph of the pope.

"Oh Cal, you're sweet. That will make me so happy."

Cal lit the candle. Gradually, slowly but faster, the four angels went around, making a very merry sound.

"Don't burn the pope!"

Cal moved the candle and angels to one side. Frannie turned off the light. The room was dark except for the candle, brass angels, and the pope's face. A little bit of light trailed in from the lodge at the north end of Duck Island.

"How romantic," Frannie said.

"What shall we do?"

"What did Father Leszinski tell us?"

"Oh yeah, right."

"Stay here Cal. I'm going to take a shower."

She took off her wedding dress and hung it just inside the open window over First Avenue. She took off her shoes.

"Now, don't peek."

She took off her slip and panties.

She went into the bathroom. There was a sound of the hot water running. She soaped and rinsed her hair, her body, her arms, everywhere. She put on the white terry cloth robe that Little Brother had given her and went back into the room after drying herself. She gave a Sienkiewicz grin to Cal.

"Do you like it, Cal?"

"It's terrific. What does the G stand for?"

"That's my middle name, Gail. Your turn to shower Cal."

Cal stood slowly, took off his tuxedo coat and trousers, and hung them next to Frannie's wedding dress. They danced in a calm breeze in front of the window, making a slight ruffling noise.

Cal took off his shoes and socks and then went into the bathroom where the hot water was still running.

"Oh Christ, that feels very good," he said.

He turned off the shower, toweled himself, put on his dry briefs, put a towel around his middle, and returned to Frannie.

He sat carefully next to her on the edge of the bed. He was trembling, and so was she.

She closed the door. Cal patted her on the thigh. She was breathing hard.

"Cal, I confess, I'm still scared."

"Frannie, I confess, I'm also still scared, but let's sit here quietly holding hands and see if we relax."

Ten minutes later, they were still nervous.

"Cal, what are we going to do?" Frannie said.

Cal stood up, took two capsules from a shirt pocket, put one in his mouth, swallowed it, and gave the other to Frannie, who looked suspiciously at the capsule.

"What are these?" she said

"These are the extremely mild tranquilizer Lorazepam I was given in the hospital and the men's shelter."

"How can I trust you, Cal?"

He bit one in half and showed Frannie.

"I wouldn't give you drugs, Frannie. I took one, and I wouldn't take weird drugs at a time like this, would I?"

"I wouldn't know what you might do at a time like this, Cal."

"This is a hell of a way to start a marriage. If you don't want it, don't take it," he said.

"If I take it, will you do abnormal things to me?"

"What the priest showed us was pretty abnormal."

"That's different. That's God's work."

"Maybe this is God's work." Cal got closer to Frannie and said softly, "I hate to see you distrust me."

She blinked a few times and then swallowed the half capsule and put the other half in her robe. After a while, she said, "I don't feel a thing."

"No, you won't for ten or fifteen minutes."

"What will I feel after?"

"Natural."

After a while, Cal put his arm around her shoulder again. She did not stiffen or resist.

"You're feeling better," Cal said.

"Oh yes," Frannie said. She leaned softly against Cal's shoulder and grinned. It was the Sienkiewicz grin. *"Let's take off our clothes,"* she whispered.

Before Cal could move, Frannie took off her terry cloth robe. She covered her private parts. Cal moved her hands away.

"Oh, little pink-white hairs."

"I'm a red head, Cal." Frannie said.

"I didn't know what to expect. I still don't."

Cal dropped his underpants to the floor, keeping his back to her.

"Turn around," Frannie said. "Am I the only one naked here?"

Cal slowly, with his hand on his private parts, turned around. He took his hands away.

"Oh my god, what's that?"

"Surely you've seen your brothers in the shower."

"Not like that. It's too big, Cal. I'm afraid it will hurt me."

She began humping. She had not willed it. She had not thought about it. It just happened. It frightened Cal. He rolled her over to her side to slow her down, but it was too late. There was a deep pulse deep within Frannie that she hadn't willed. It just happened.

"... Oh!"

Cal put her on her tummy and, with his right arm, lifted her slightly so that she was on her knees.

"No Cal, not like that. We have to do it the way the priest showed us."

Cal put her on her back and re-entered.

The Christmas music played gently and sweetly. Cal was afraid nothing was going to happen for him.

"I'm afraid nothing will happen."

Very softly, the door to the house opened, and they could hear Joey and Little Brother stumbling in. Cal was very timid now, so he was going slowly. He felt a restraining hand on the back of his neck.

"Joey?"

But it wasn't Joey or Little Brother. To get it over with, Cal went faster and faster. "Oh," he said, "I'm a machine!"

Joey was drunk. Little Brother pushed him upstairs. When they got to Frannie's bedroom door, Little Brother banged on it and said, "Ok, you guys, we're home, stop whatever you're doing ... Hold the banister Joey. I can hold you a little bit, but not if you fall backward." Their voices trailed off into the uppermost bedroom.

Cal suddenly felt luxuriously sleepy and lowered his head to Frannie's face. He lay there. Frannie was still breathing rapidly but was slowing down, and her face was flushed. The candle was almost guttering out now.

Cal got up and moved the candle to the far end of the dresser. Frannie sat on the far edge of the bed against the wall with a blanket delicately across her privates and an arm across her breasts.

"I didn't do very well, did I?" Cal said.

"It was our first time, Cal."

"I shouldn't have taken that tranquilizer."

"No."

"But it didn't slow you down, did it Frannie?"

"No," Frannie laughed, "not at all." She laughed again.

Gentle snores came from the bedroom above.

Cal walked to the open window.

"You should cross yourself when passing the portrait of His Holiness," she said.

Cal walked back to the dresser, crossed himself, then went back to the window. The lodge sparkled from the bridge lights and the downtown lights. A few bare trees glimmered. He heard the sound of Big Bull Falls.

"Where is Wilkins now?"

"Come here, Cal. I want to do it again."

"Let's kill ourselves."

"What?"

"Never mind, come here. I want to show you something on Duck Island."

She wrapped herself in the blanket, got off the bed, and joined Cal at the window.

"You see all those white fish at the edge of the west channel? I wonder if they're dead."

She hauled him back to bed, took off her blanket, and lay on her back.

"Climb aboard, engineer. You're still hot, Cal."

"Not really."

"Well, let's try anyway."

Cal went as fast as he could, but nothing happened for him. She put her hands on his bare buttocks and softly pulled inward. Finally, he gave up. They closed their eyes and slept, his arm over her stomach. When Cal opened his eyes, the far window showed purple to the east.

"Frannie, let's go down and greet the dawn."

"What shall we wear?"

"Oh, our wedding outfits for sure."

"Yes!"

They dressed quickly, she in her patchwork wedding dress and he in the black tuxedo. They went downstairs. Little Brother was in the living room with their father's accordion. He played slowly and sadly "Do Not Forsake Me O' My Darling". He played a little bit louder as they came down the stairs. He put the accordion down and went over to kiss Frannie.

"I will never forsake you, Little Brother," she said.

"That's what you say. That's not what you did."

Little Brother left.

Cal and Frannie knelt at the altar and prayed in gratitude to the Holy Mother of God. They got up. Frannie opened the pantry door and went outside. Her wedding dress rustled gently. "It's warm," she said.

Cal, still in the kitchen, took out a grooved red pill from his back pocket and a little bit of water and swallowed it. Frannie came back. Cal held out another grooved red pill to her.

"What's that?"

"For you, or don't you trust me?"

"Of course I trust you."

She put the pill in her mouth, took some water from Cal's glass, and swallowed. Suddenly, her eyes widened, and she stared at Cal.

"That wasn't poison, was it?" she said.

"Poison? Who said anything about poison?"

"Well, you said something kind of weird last night when you were at the window."

Purple glints of the Wisconsin River came through branches with red buds. Cal and Frannie crossed the railroad tracks and went onto the pale concrete bridge.

Down below was the Junior Game Warden Lodge. She put her arm around Cal's back.

"That's where we met! We'll have to have a memorial plaque put on the second floor."

"No, we met at the Jesus house."

Suddenly, a large school of silvery fish slithered across the Wisconsin River to the east.

They walked a little bit more on the bridge.

Chapter 28

Frannie started to step backwards across the bridge.

"Stay there, Cal." She tried to throw up, but nothing would come, even when she put her finger down her throat.

"Where are you going?" Cal yelled.

Frannie kept trying to throw up as she walked.

"I want an annulment!"

"What's that?"

"Look it up, stupid!"

"Don't call me stupid! Frannie, I love you!! I need you!" Cal cried out.

"No, you don't! I hope you got what you came for!"

Frannie walked past a silo for Robin Hood Flour. It had a painting on the corrugated walls of a medieval English long-bow archer. Wherever Frannie moved, the arrow was aimed at her heart.

The roof of the Duck Island Junior Game Warden Lodge began to sink until it was concave, and steam rose from it.

Frannie clung to her golden cross and said softly, "Oh Jesus, help me, help me." She stumbled forward.

The white fish in a row along the west side of the west channel bore circular scars from lampreys, large open mouths studded with extremely sharp teeth.

They began to drift away under the old white bridge to the end of Duck Island, where they joined the main stream in the direction of Stevens Point, where abnormal orange clouds were rising.

A big black bull humped a wooden fence at the top of Big Bull Falls. Finally, he ejaculated and fell.

Frannie stumbled around the corner heading for the eastern hills.

"I'll tell Joey... I'll tell Joey... I'll tell Joey..." Frannie said.

Cal walked up to Stone Street past the men's shelter and Von Gnechten bakery. The sun was too bright to look at. Eastern Wausau turned deep red. Cal turned the corner and headed west on Third Street past the Hotel Wausau and on past La Cantina and Gowns by Carole.

"Big deal," Cal said.

"He's going to kill you ... He's going to kill you ... He's going to kill you," she mumbled, going east, uphill, "and I'll help him."

A horned goat with a black rosary around its neck trampled blue irises. There was a stone wishing well. It was open topped. Black snakes crawled around its bottom, spitting venom. A bird, neither eagle nor hawk, but with talons, swooped down to one of the snakes, shot up high into the air, and then dropped the wriggling reptile into the wishing well, at the bottom of which was a pink cockatoo.

Cal went under the Grand Avenue marquee on the right. He cried some more.

"Oh Wausau, Wausau, what happened to you?"

A ladder leaned against the white marquee where red letters had been placed which were still unreadable, but the posters were already up. Kirk Douglas, bare chested and with gritted teeth, hauled a harpoon behind his right ear, ready to throw it into the eye of a giant squid that had already wrapped its tentacles around the *Nautilus*. Suddenly there was a BOOM BOOM BOOM. A rowboat lost its moorings and floated into the middle of the Wisconsin River. Nobody was in it. Ojibwa hauled transparent canoes onto Duck Island. They stepped out and formed a circle. Several Ojibwas plucked dry twigs for kindling and let them fall for firewood. Another Indian, not Ojibwe, went around the circle of seated natives and filled each man's pipe with tobacco. Slowly, luxuriously, men smoked. Because they were transparent, they faded away. There was nobody on Duck Island.

Chapter 29

Cal turned. A stream of red lobsters crawled up toward Third Street.

Clackety clack clackety clack.

Cal stepped back onto some green grass, filled with hordes of starfish without arms or legs. He hurried on.

The drug began losing its potency.

Cal crossed Grand Avenue and went west until he came to the red granite obelisks and red granite tombstones of the Christian graveyard. The sun had risen by now and was very bright in the east and was shining on many red granite polished tombstones.

The sun topped the peak of the obelisks and spread its rays over the Christians, their ferns, their crosses, and their prayers.

Cal crossed himself, then jogged across Grand Avenue. A pickup truck with a rifle in a gun rack inside the cabin slammed on its brakes. A red convertible Ford with a black cloth top slammed into the pickup truck's rear. It smashed the license, the rear lights, the fender, and a good part of the pickup truck's body. The drivers got out to discuss the matter. Cal looked up and down the next lane. It was clear. He jogged to the far sidewalk where a Hmong jabbed his forefinger, pointing and laughing at the two drivers punching each other in the middle of Grand Avenue, stopping traffic both ways.

"Americans," the Hmong said.

Cal ducked under part of the green pole fence into the Hebrew graveyard.

"Leila Tov," the Hmong said.

Cal froze for a second and said "Leila Tov," then went on across the damp green law. Other mourners walked slowly on the flagstone path into the graveyard.

He found his father's gravestone in the shade of rustling evergreen trees.

It was a gray stone inscribed with a large six-pointed Jewish star. Cal fingered out the frost in the lines of the Jewish star and also in the letters of the words below:

Samuel Bedrick
Chemistry Professor, University Wisconsin
Born in Duluth, Minnesota
Died in Atlanta, Georgia

The pines fluttered in a quick breeze. He plucked off some pine needles and autumn leaves that had fallen on the top of the tombstone. He brushed aside debris at the base of the tombstone.

Cal took out a crumpled newspaper article. It was by Margaret Carstens, the social editor.

"Peter Sluzarski won the Samuel Bedrick Chemistry Scholarship of $1,000," he read.

He put the newspaper back in his pocket.

"You know for sure that Mom went there, maybe she presented the scholarship award to Peter at the front of the stage. I'm sure Clarke was there too. Oh yes, I almost forgot, I'm wearing a tuxedo because yesterday I married a Catholic girl. I'm very sorry about that, Dad, but if you knew her you'd understand."

After a long while he turned and walked out of the Hebrew graveyard. He walked back on the wet green grass to the sidewalk and went west.

He passed an Esso station that had been leased by Mr. Brecker, Sr. Brecker, Jr. had been one of Cal's best friends, but he had died. After the gas station was demolished, there was nothing left of the gas pumps. There were just rectangular holes in the ground that the city had been foaming. The brown clapboard house had been demolished, and the apple tree cut down. No more chess. Mr. and Mrs. Brecker had been unable to save any money, but they sold their franchise and moved to a modern house in the Township of Rib Mountain, beyond Lake Wausau. They could see an apple tree and Rib Mountain through the kitchen window. In the winter, neighborhood boys shoveled their sidewalk, walkway, and garage driveway in return for Mrs. Brecker's homemade Bavarian Christmas cookies. Mr. and Mrs. Brecker's hair turned white, and since the shades were always drawn, the light in the house looked sickly yellow which the monthly social security checks never quite alleviated.

Cal kept walking, into the contiguous township of Schofield, past the Arvold Plywood Factory. On the right side was a Tastee Freez. Cal went to the counter of the Tastee Freez, where a young man with a white shirt, curly red hair, and a server's cap was working behind the counter. It was Jerry Szabo.

"Hey, you're Cal Bedrick. You got married yesterday. Where's Frannie? I was in the church when you got married. What happened? Couldn't you do it?"

"Nothing like that, I made a little mistake, and now she will annul the marriage."

"Where is she?"

"I don't know. She doesn't know. God doesn't know."

"I'm really sorry to hear this."

They looked at each other. It was clear what Cal wanted.

"I was born in Wausau, I grew up in Wausau, left Wausau, and then came back to Wausau. Now I'm leaving Wausau again. I'm so hungry. I have no money. Could I please have an ice cream cone or something?"

Jerry shook his head, "We're not supposed to do that sort of thing."

They stared at each other's eyes.

"One day, you will be hungry," Cal said.

The young man hesitated, then went back to a chrome ice milk dispenser, pulled the handle down, and turned an empty cone, making a swirl of white milk ice cream on top. Then, with his other hand, he lifted a hotdog bun, opened it with his left hand, and reached into a revolving heater. The ice milk was done. He took the hotdog to the front of the Tastee Freez in a serrated paper container and sat the ice cream next to it.

"Your order, sir. Ketchup and mayo on the picnic bench over there. Do you want a pickle?" Jerry said.

"No."

Cal wolfed down the hotdog. He licked the ice cream cone. Jerry motioned him to the window to pick up a napkin when he was through. He dabbed at Cal's mouth.

"If I was you, Mr. Bedrick, I'd go back and find that girl. Don't let her out of your sight. She is a gem."

Cal threw the hotdog holder into the top of the metal swing bin waste container, which he missed. Mustard and ketchup fell to the ground.

"I'll take care of it, I always do," Jerry said. "No matter how poor I get I will never beg for food."

Jerry came out and around the waste container and mopped up the stains.

Cal began to walk west down Highway 29. The grass was sweet and green. The sun was warm. After a while, Cal turned and stuck out his thumb. A trucker stopped and opened the cab door. Cal got in and closed the door.

"Where are you going?" The truck driver said.

"Oregon."

Chapter 30

"Existence has lost all its reality… oh. how horrible."

Two badgers copulated on a mound of leaves. A doe stepped timidly on a lawn.

"Oh lady deer, where is your husband? Has he deceived you, too?" Frannie said.

She kept stumbling forward until she came to an intersection of 76th Street crossing 76th Avenue. It was so bright she could hardly see.

Frannie held out her left hand. "Won't anybody lend me a hand?" she said.

There were two bright white clapboard churches next to each other. One of the churches was letting people out. The pastor was dressed informally in a check shirt and blue trousers. He touched everyone on the back in a very gentle and friendly way.

Frannie stared at him.

"Are you lost?" The pastor said.

"Yes."

He smiled and said, "We are all lost from time to time … I was lost until I found God and became a preacher. What are you looking for, young lady?"

"My home."

"Where is your home?"

"Duck Island."

"Well, if it's an island, it must be on the river."

"Yes."

"Well, then you must go downhill, and I advise you to go back the way you came before you go downhill."

"Thank you. You're very kind. Who are you?"

He bowed gently and put his thumb and forefingers together to make a circle on his chest. "We are the Moravian Brethren."

Frannie stumbled down the way she had come until she came to the Klein house. Joshua sat on a webbed garden chair reading Nietzsche. Frannie turned away from the path and went downhill towards the forest. She pointed at Joshua.

"Evil. Evil. Evil."

She walked downhill through toadstools, ferns unfurling, and branches. She tripped over one and fell to her knees.

"Jesus."

She got up and walked until she could hear Big Bull Falls down below. She came out across from the main Wausau Hotel. She crossed the road and opened the door. Customers stared at her.

"Are you lost?" a man said.

"I want to go home."

The man stood up. "I can drive you home."

"I'm not getting into a car with a man," Frannie said, then left the hotel.

She passed the bakery, which was still closed. She knocked on the men's shelter door, which was still closed. Mr. Dula opened the door.

"Frannie! What happened to you?"

"I want to go home."

"You're not well, Frannie."

"I want to go home."

"I'll escort you."

"No. I'll go down the other way."

She left the men's shelter and went to the next street. She went under the Lemke sign, "From Moo to You in an Hour or Two", and across from the former Employers Mutual headquarters.

Frannie stepped onto the black railroad trestle bridge. She was halfway across when she heard the two-toned horn blast of a train coming behind her very fast.

It was bright yellow with broad diagonal green stripes. It was hooked to a second similar diesel engine facing backward. It was carrying chunks of coal.

The horn blasted again. She looked back. The train could not possibly stop in time, and there was no room for her to run straight ahead.

The engineer waved violently to the side of the bridge. Frannie backed all the way into the black iron wall, crossed herself, and lifted the gold cross on her neck to kiss it.

"Sweet Jesus, keep me from the flames of hell."

The train roared by. A tornado of black coal dust covered Frannie.

"Oh, my wedding dress. It's soiled!" She wept.

When the train passed, she picked up a chunk of coal and threw it at the departing engine. She had a strong arm and was accurate. The coal chunk struck the front window of the train facing backward. The train driver shook a gloved fist at her and then was gone, leaving a red light. Frannie went to the far end of the bridge and looked at her house with its oil portrait of Jesus over the white wooden kitchen table. Little Brother had enlisted by now. Joey's Datsun truck was gone.

She went down the long muddy path to the old white bridge over the flooded western channel. She sloshed across to the Junior Game Warden Lodge and pounded on the door, which was locked.

"Cal! Cal, are you there?" She kicked the door "Cal!" she started to cry.

She turned, slipped down the wet wooden stairs, and fell onto a mound of muddy grass which further blackened her wedding dress. The island was flooded up to two feet. The reflection of bare or budding trees wiggled and waggled on the water. She crawled forward on her stomach and stopped on a tiny mound of snow.

"Helpmehelpmehelpme."

A fisherman with hip-high brown rubber waders put his fishing rod against a bridge post and sloshed through to Frannie. "Oh lady, what's wrong? Have you hurt yourself? Let me help you up."

He reached under her armpits and held her up, so she was standing. Her eyes were not focused.

"We have to get out of Duck Island," she said.

He put his arm around her waist. Together they trudged back over the old white wooden bridge and went up the slippery, muddy path to the roads above. When they got to the top, Frannie looked at her home across First Avenue. It was completely dark. Nobody. Nothing. No Cal, no Joey, and no Little Brother, who had taken the oath into the US armed forces and was undoubtedly on a Greyhound bus headed for the barracks far away.

"You're homeless, aren't you?" the fisherman said. He turned her around and pressed his middle against her middle. Frannie was still strong. She pushed him backward so hard that he fell onto his back and slithered down the path left, right, left, right, all the way to the old white wooden bridge, banging his head on the bridge post, which he grabbed for dear life to keep from going into the swollen waters.

"Jesus Christ!"

Frannie ran across Stewart Avenue. A car swerved and narrowly missed her. Frannie came to Third Avenue and went to the Piggly Wiggly, which was still closed and dark. Frannie left and went up to Fourth Avenue. She stopped a lady with shopping bags and asked the lady, "Can you please tell me, where is Jesus?"

The woman stared at Frannie's muddy wedding dress and shoes and backed away. "I'm sure I don't know," she said, then left.

An old man with a white cane stopped four feet in front of her, took off a hat, and bowed. "How may I be of assistance?" he asked.

"I'm looking for Jesus."

"We all are," the old man said. "Judging by your cross, I assume you are Catholic. There is a Catholic church one more block down Fourth and to the right." He bowed and tottered on to Stewart.

Frannie found her church. A double row of tulips had been planted under the rosette window. The door was locked. Frannie pounded on and kicked the door.

"Father Leszinski! Father Petrus!"

She went down to the basement door. It was also locked.

"Sister Elizabeth!"

She pounded and kicked. Nobody came to open the door.

Frannie cried.

She crossed the river and went down Grand Avenue. She took no notice of any shops or the movie theater. She stopped at a bus stop in front of the dark La Cantina. Nobody was inside. The sun had gone down in the west. She waited. Flat clouds in the east had turned silver, white. It was so bright there were no stars, but the moon rose. It was full and silver, white. It came over the lawn leading to the music stage and brightened it and the paths leading to it and the grass where the rest of downtown had once been.

She waited.

A car stopped. "There's no bus until dawn. Can I give you a lift?" the man driving it said.

Frannie did not answer. The car drove off. The moon went brightly over the Wisconsin River and finally began settling in the west. The flat clouds in the far east turned pink yellow. Slowly the sun began to rise.

A municipal bus came down Grand Avenue. Frannie held out her right hand. The bus stopped right in front of her. The front door unfolded.

"I can't take you on this bus, miss. You're too dirty. You've got mud all over you. Front and back. Where are you going anyway?"

Frannie gave him a Sienkiewicz smile.

"I'm going home to Jesus."